salt in the wound

SIERRA SIMONE

a quick note

This story was supposed to be short.

Like, really short.

I thought it would be fun to write about Mark and Isolde meeting, how their arranged marriage actually gets arranged, maybe some spanking.

You know, typical Sierra stuff.

Five to ten thousand words, I told myself. Just a little niblet of these two monsters—well, one monster and one fledgling monster—getting together.

And…somehow I wrote a whole book instead.

I'd like to make it clear that this isn't my fault—this is Mark and Isolde's collective fault. They climbed into my brain and made it theirs, and what was supposed to be a fun little bonus story is now forty-eight thousand words of a devil and the bride he bartered for.

And of course, a very important moment at the end, which sets up the entire Lyonesse[1] trilogy.

I hope you enjoy our kinky devil and his stabby Isolde, and if you do, there is plenty of Mark Trevena (and Isolde and horny, horny Tristan) in the (official) first book of the Lyonesse trilogy, Salt Kiss!

1. Lyonesse is the name of the drowned kingdom off the Cornish coast that features prominently in the Tristan and Isolde stories. Eagle-eyed readers from the New Camelot series will spot it as the name of the kink club where Ash learns how to be a Dominant.

content warning

This story contains mentions of self-harm in a religious context[1] and its relation to kink.

---

1. The practice of corporal penance.

Blessed be the Lord, my rock,
  who trains my hands for battle,
  my fingers for war...

PSALM 144:1

one

I was seventeen when I met the devil.

Sister Mary Alice had just given us our first knives—training knives, made of black rubber which bent if you pressed too hard—and Bryn and I were sparring. Not that it could be called that, even charitably, because we were too nervous to actually strike at each other. The knives might have been made of rubber, but the *idea* of the knives was real enough to make us shy.

Bryn and I had been training in the sisters' dojo since we were twelve. Six days a week I was on its old red carpet or its beaten blue mats, sweating, pushing, kicking, punching. There was sparring, self-defense, katas. Rattan canes and wooden swords when we'd turned fifteen, and bo staffs later on. We weren't afraid of hitting each other, and we weren't afraid of getting hit.

But there was something about the knives.

The bell above the door rang. Bryn and I had grown up hearing that bell and so we didn't bother looking. No one ever came to this place who didn't mean to come to this place. The entrance to the sisters' dojo was two stories below, a black door squashed between a parking garage and a thrift store. It didn't even have a sign above it, only the number of a Bible verse painted in faint green letters.

Psalm 144:1. Which if you flipped to in the Bible, would read:

Blessed be the Lord, my rock,
who trains my hands for battle,
my fingers for war.

The sisters' school didn't have a name that I knew of, they had never even attempted a website, and their phone was an ancient thing made of yellowed plastic that I only saw answered once. People came through the door because they were delivering something or because they were supposed to be here, and that was it.

So it wasn't until Bryn got past her nerves and finally made her first strike that I saw him.

Tall and broad-shouldered. A suit too nice for this place. Too nice for a lot of places, actually.

And he was watching us.

I turned back to Bryn, and she lifted a shoulder before settling into a sparring stance. She didn't know who he was either.

Awareness prickled along the back of my neck as I tried to focus on the sparring, on the tip of Bryn's fake knife.

What is it about being watched that makes us want to impress the watcher? I didn't know him; I didn't need to prove anything to him. And yet when Bryn managed to wedge her knife against my armpit, I was embarrassed. Tried even harder, only for her to catch me a third time with her blade.

A throat cleared.

I turned to see the man standing several paces away, his jacket off and his feet bare on the old red carpet. He was rolling up his sleeves to expose sun-bronzed forearms, his fingers working the fabric in quick, deft rolls. A wristwatch glinted, expensive but not ostentatious, which probably meant it was even more expensive than it looked.

"May I?" he asked, extending his hand, palm up, to Bryn. His voice was deep and rough and cold. Ice wouldn't melt in that voice. But it was mannerly, polite.

Some devils hide, you see. Right in plain sight.

I watched then as Bryn placed her knife on his palm. We were used to being shown what we were doing wrong—any martial arts teacher did that—but our teachers were Catholic, so we were doubly blessed in that regard. We were trained to be excellent students. Trained never to miss a chance to learn.

But still. He was a stranger in a place that never had strangers. I might have refused on those grounds alone. Yet I faced him and bowed, just as he did to me. I shifted my weight until I was light on my feet and supple as a willow branch in the wind. And I watched as he didn't shift at all.

I was so very aware of everything as I stepped to the side. Of the sweat between my palm and the rubber hilt of the knife, of where my gi jacket gaped open to expose my throat and collarbone. Of the heavy blond ponytail brushing against the back of my gi as I moved, a slow drag across the cotton. I allowed my awareness to expand to him, to his easy, upright posture, to the way he held his knife backwards, the blade coming from the outside of his fist rather than the inside. I'd only ever seen people hold a knife like that in movies.

I remember that I thought he was *almost* handsome that day. He had a strong nose, with a flare at the bridge which told me it had been broken before. He had a jaw straight out of my AP geometry textbook, shadowed with rough stubble. A high forehead with a thin scar furrowing into his dark blond hair, straight, thick brows, and dark blue eyes.

A mouth with a precisely formed upper lip and a curved lower one, which somehow gave the impression of softness and firmness at once.

I know now he was only in his early thirties, but at the

time, he was in the same category as all adults to me—teachers, doctors, presidents, uncles, nuns, whatever.

There was only young and old. I was young. He was not.

But despite that, he moved easier than anyone I'd ever seen, including my teachers. As I stepped lightly in the almost-dance of sparring, he walked normally, his shoulders relaxed and his hands at his sides. To the uninitiated, it might look like he was asking for an attack by not having his guards up, by not having his knife out. Even then, I knew better. He never crossed a foot in front of the other as he walked; the looseness of his shoulders and arms meant he could snap into motion at any moment. He was baiting me, maybe. Or simply waiting for me to move.

Fine then. I could move. I'd been doing this almost my entire life, was the best at my school, and I wasn't wearing impeccably tailored trousers like he was—

Before my knife hand had even made it an inch, I was blocked, seized, spun. By the time I registered what was happening, my back was to his chest and his knife was to my throat.

His chest was warm even through my gi jacket and the tank top I wore underneath. His arms around me were an iron cage, and the rubber knife to my throat pressed just hard enough to make me lift my chin. I didn't smell cologne or any other kind of expensive scent, which seemed unusual for someone who would go to the trouble to wear such a nice suit; instead, I only smelled fresh and clean air, soap, perhaps, and something else underneath it. The way the air smells after rain, maybe.

He only held me there an instant, long enough to make his point, short enough to be sportsmanlike.

Still. I had no intention of repeating that particular humiliation.

But when I turned to tell him so, I saw Sister Mary Alice and Sister Grace watching me from the dojo's front desk, their arms crossed. Sister Mary Alice lifted a pale, calloused hand from where it had been tucked into her elbow.

The message was clear. I was to continue.

I kept my breathing even and focused on settling my energy back into my belly.

"How long have you had that knife?" he asked as we bowed and started again. Like the last time, he merely walked while I danced around him—but now I knew the speed and strength that little deception of his hid.

"An hour," I told him.

"They only showed you standard grip, I presume?"

"They didn't show me anything. They wanted us to get a feel for them before we started formal lessons."

He nodded again, and then tucked his tie into his shirt with his free hand. With a flick of his fingers, he was holding the knife like me. "This is standard grip," he said. "Sometimes called a hammer grip. You can move your thumb to a saber grip, like so, but that's still really just standard grip when you consider the direction of the blade."

I braced my thumb on the edge of the hilt like he did, and then slid it back. "Okay," I said quietly. I wasn't sure why he was teaching me this, or why we were even sparring in the first place, but I was hungry to learn, desperate to push myself.

"This," the stranger said, flipping the knife and then catching it expertly with the blade pointing down, "is reverse grip."

"Like a serial killer," Bryn chirped from over by the mirrors.

A corner of the stranger's mouth pressed in, faintly. "Yes. And now it's easier to use my fist as a fist if I need to. Now I have more leverage for slicing, and more force for stabbing."

I followed his lead and changed my own grip to reverse. It felt strange—it wasn't the way you'd first think to hold a knife

—but it felt powerful too. I could feel how much faster I could cut, how much harder I could stab.

"Good," he said, and when he said *good* in that rough, cold voice, something flickered in my chest, in my thoughts, gone before I could really perceive it. "Now, do you see the difference?"

"Standard is blade up," I answered, "and reverse is blade down."

A shake of his head. "Standard," he said slowly, "is for a fair fight. But reverse?" Once again, he moved faster than I could stop him. This time I landed on my back, with him on top of me. The tip of his rubber blade was lodged against my windpipe. "Reverse is for when you mean it," he finished.

I blinked up at him, too stunned for the humiliation to sink in, although it would dig its teeth into me later. In a fast, graceful movement, he was standing, and then he grabbed my forearm and pulled me to my feet.

He dropped my arm as soon as I had my balance and then crossed the space to return the knife to Bryn. She and I watched as he strode over to the area by the door and put on his socks and shoes with elegant, efficient movements. Sister Mary Alice and Sister Grace were gone.

"Well, Isolde," the stranger said as he stood up. His sleeves were still rolled up and his jacket was slung over his forearm. "It was lovely meeting you."

He left, the bell on the door ringing long after it had shut.

I turned to face Bryn, who was still staring at the door he'd walked through. When she swiveled her head to look at me, there was a question written all over her tan, heart-shaped face.

"How did he know your name?" she asked.

two

T he first time I sensed things weren't entirely as they seemed was three months after I met the stranger in the dojo. It was my senior year of high school, and my father—who split his time between London and New York —had brought me to our Kensington terrace for my winter break. Professionally designed Christmas decorations filled the corners and twined up stair railings. The tall Georgian rooms were filled with fresh evergreens and bowls of baubles and twinkling candles lit by staff. Piles of presents, neatly wrapped, beckoned from under the tree. My father hadn't bought any of them for me. I doubted he even knew what they were. Something as unimportant as presents was undoubtedly delegated to the same person who sent me birthday cards when he was out of town, and who arranged for the driver to pick me up from school.

We ate a late Christmas Eve dinner in the too-grand dining room, candlelight glinting off the hand-painted china. It was just the two of us; my mother was long dead by then. There'd only been two of us at Christmas dinner for the past five years, and yet that empty spot at the table was still so full of my mother's absence that it ached like a tooth.

"Your school report was quite good," my father said. Despite being uninterested in the minutiae of parenting a teenager, Geoffrey Laurence took a keen interest in *me*. He expected the best from me, which I was grateful for. Even if sometimes I wasn't exactly sure what he wanted beyond good grades and impeccable manners.

But surely he wanted what I also wanted; he'd never said otherwise. He'd allowed me to spend as much time as I wanted at the dojo, he'd never contradicted me when I spoke of my plans for the future. He'd never seemed jealous that I'd idolized my maternal uncle, a cardinal in the Catholic Church, more than I had him, Geoffrey Laurence, king of bankers.

"Thank you," I answered politely.

My father took a bite of goose, chewed, cut off another bite. "And you are still committed to Columbia?" He didn't look at me as he spoke.

"Yes," I said, "but—"

I didn't have a chance to raise the issue of my major, because just then a tall man strode into the room, the scarlet-trimmed hem of his simar fluttering around gleaming shoes. His cheeks above his neatly shorn beard were freckled, ruddy, dotted with pockmarks, and when he smiled at me, the smile revealed a gap between his front teeth. Flurries dusted the black cape hanging over his shoulders.

He held out his arms in welcome, and getting up to answer the invitation for a hug was as natural as breathing. My uncle Mortimer was as warm as my father was cold, and the only adult in my life who truly understood what I wanted after school.

"I didn't know you were coming," I said into Mortimer's chest. The chain of his gold pectoral cross pressed into my cheek before I pulled away to beam at him. "I thought you'd be in Rome."

"I had business in London tonight," he said, giving my

shoulder a fond pat. The Irish in his voice had been sanded down by years of living at the Holy See, but the lilt was still there. It reminded me of my mother's voice. "But it's concluded now. So I thought I'd come check on my favorite niece."

"Your only niece," I reminded him as I went back to my place at the table. Mortimer sat without an invitation from my father and gave the both of us another wide smile, the gap in his teeth flashing.

"I hope I'm not intruding," he said.

"Of course you aren't intruding—"

"Isolde," my father interrupted sharply. "Go to your room."

I froze, my fingers stalled in the act of reaching for my fork. "I'm sorry?"

Geoffrey Laurence turned his dark eyes on me. His already thin mouth was pressed even thinner, the lines bracketing his mouth severe. "I need to speak to your uncle. Please leave us."

I looked over to my uncle, whose wide smile was still on his face. "Don't worry, Isolde. It won't take but a minute."

I nodded and stood, leaving my napkin on the chair and walking out of the dining room and up the stairs to my own room. Where I promptly slipped off my shoes and then crept back to the stairs, careful to descend along the sturdy, quiet edges, rolling my bare foot from ball to toes with each silent step until I was at the bottom and within earshot of the dining room.

"It's as good as done," my father was saying. His English voice was as crisp and cool as money, a banker's voice. "And it serves us both, as you well know."

"Perhaps."

I knew Mortimer's cryptic response would infuriate my father, because it would be coupled with Mortimer's famous arched eyebrow, that gap-toothed smile. My uncle *handled*

SIERRA SIMONE

things for the Vatican, and there were many reasons why he was indispensable to the Vatican, but one very important reason was his inscrutability. He gave nothing away that he didn't want to.

"I know what you're thinking," my father said, and I'd been right, I could hear the defensiveness in his words.

My uncle's voice was a raspy one, a voice that always had a sense of wheezing to it, and so when he pitched his voice low and quiet, like he did just then, I couldn't make him out from my position on the stairs. That voice was part of what made him so good at Vatican diplomacy, he'd once told me. He could be extremely difficult to eavesdrop on when he wanted to be.

But I could make out the last bit of what he said.

"…would be a waste, Geoffrey."

"For you, maybe," replied my father.

Once again, my uncle was difficult to make out. But I thought I heard the word *weapon*, which couldn't be right.

"I don't want to be at odds with you on this, so I hope you'll reconsider," my father answered tightly. China clinked and a chair scraped—someone was standing abruptly. Perhaps readying to leave the room.

With a light movement, I leapt back up the stairs, just as quietly as I'd come down. I was fast, and a few minutes later, when my uncle knocked on my door, I was at my desk reading in a settled position, not a hair out of place.

"Come in," I called, and he let himself in, a pillar of clerical black in my spare, cream-colored room.

"Very good," he said as he sat down in a small armchair near my bookshelves. "I didn't hear you at all."

I dipped my chin in acknowledgment. It had been him who'd taught me how to creep, eavesdrop, how to listen unperceived. As a child, he would send me around parties and events, and I'd be his ears for him. His ears on a quiet little girl no one thought to curb their words around.

10

Have any crumbs for me, little mouse? he used to ask, and I would give him any crumbs he wished for, my smiling uncle who carried me on his shoulders and taught me how to pray so that God would listen. As I got older, the crumbs became larger, gathering them more dangerous. And so he'd schooled me over the years, and it had become second nature to gather the information he wanted, to sneak into places I wasn't meant to be, and to hide in plain sight in the places I *was* supposed to be.

"What were you talking about?" Mortimer was the one person other than Bryn and my confessor that I was entirely candid with, and he'd encouraged my curiosity from the moment I could talk. When other adults ignored my questions or batted them away with canned answers, Mortimer listened to them, took them seriously. And whenever I asked something that he wouldn't—or couldn't—answer, he apologized sincerely.

In a perfect world, we know all things, Isolde. Alas that this isn't a perfect world—yet.

From the way he smiled at my question, I knew I wasn't getting an answer tonight.

"I wish I could tell you, but your father has asked me not to."

Alarm, cold and tight, pulled at my stomach for a moment. I ignored it. "So it's about me."

Mortimer nodded. "I'm afraid so."

"Is it about my future? About my vocation?"

Mortimer didn't hesitate. "Yes."

I looked down at the book in my hands, St. Ignatius's *Spiritual Exercises.* "I'm not changing my plans. I want to take vows. I want to work for God. I want to work for the Church."

"My child, so you shall," my uncle said kindly. "You were marked for God from the moment you were born, and marked for increasing His glory here on Earth. You have exactly the gifts the Church needs."

"Father doesn't understand that," I said. I closed the book, smoothing the battered cover and setting it on my desk. "He wants me for the glory of the Laurence family."

It had been an ongoing argument since I'd told him the day after my mother's funeral that I wanted to become a nun. He wanted me to join the ranks of Laurence Bank, the financial empire his great-great-grandfather had founded in 1901, and the idea that his only child would throw her future away on intentional poverty had infuriated him. I'd informed him he could always have more children.

The conversation hadn't much improved from there.

"I imagine the compromise you've struck still holds," Mortimer assured me. "You'll go to university before you do anything else, and so you have time. We have time."

If only my father didn't also want me to major in something I didn't care about in the meantime. He was hoping an education in finance would help me see the value in Laurence Bank.

"I know what I'm meant to do," I said. "I'm meant to be God's hands."

"And so you shall be," Mortimer said. "I will never steer you away from what God needs you to do."

I hadn't raised the next subject for the last few months, but Mortimer's assurances made me hopeful. And, I supposed, it would be a nice Christmas present, if an unusual one.

"Have you…" I forced the words out, even though speaking one of my deepest spiritual needs aloud was like spreading my ribs apart and allowing someone to look at the bloody machinery underneath. I hated vulnerability, even with the one adult I trusted above all others.

Mortimer took pity on me. "I know what you're asking, Isolde, and yes, I have given it more thought. And my answer hasn't changed. Corporal penance is something that's rarely permissible in the eyes of the Church."

I wanted to push my ribs back together, I wanted to sew myself back up and pretend I hadn't bled in front of this man I idolized so much, but I couldn't help myself. "I wouldn't be irresponsible with it, I promise. I would do it under the direction of my confessor. I would only use it as needed—"

"The gift God is giving you now," my uncle suggested softly, "is one of deprivation. You must offer up that lack, that yearning, to him. You must live without this thing you crave to better serve him. There is no more valuable suffering or penance than that."

I swallowed. "But—"

"Isolde, you wish to be God's hands here on Earth. That requires sacrifice. You cannot creep through rooms with a cinched thigh, you cannot listen for me unnoticed at your father's galas and parties if everyone is noticing the flagellation marks on your shoulders. If you are to be God's creature as I have molded you to be, your body must be whole and strong and unmarked. You must not fast from nourishment, because it will make you weaker. You must not keep yourself awake, because it will make you slower." He reached for my hand and squeezed it. "I would not score a blade or throw it carelessly into a fire. Neither will I allow you to damage yourself when you are already consecrated to the cause."

13

three

The rest of the year passed quickly.

I went back to Manhattan and my Upper East Side prep school. I turned eighteen. I lived my days as if I were already under vows.

I prayed; I studied the Bible; I studied Greek and Latin and Hebrew. And I trained. I woke early to run, to lift, to move through my katas. After school, I sparred and punched and kicked. I used the knife until it became an extension of my own hand.

I thought often of that suited stranger and how easily he moved, how easily he'd held the knife. I aspired to that ease, and I told myself that was why I thought of him so much. And if the evocative smell of him and those midnight eyes lingered in my mind, it was only because I was preoccupied with his competence and skill.

Mercifully, my father refrained from any more complaints about my future plans, and the university truce between us held. I would still go to Columbia, and there was no mention of whatever it was he'd discussed with my uncle over Christmas.

At night, I dreamed of pain, of suffering, and when I

woke up, I was unsettled and strange-feeling. I *should* not lust. *I did not lust.* And yet when I dreamed, I woke up panting and wet between the legs. It shamed me, because my craving for corporal penance was pure and good, *I knew it*, I knew it beyond a doubt when I was awake. But when I was asleep, my cravings for pain became dark and strange to me. As if my body were no longer under my control.

Bryn and I graduated from high school, and as always, I dedicated the summer after to training, giving little thought to Columbia and the change that lay ahead. School was nothing but a concession for me, a necessary pretense until I could convince my father that my future lay with the Church and my uncle, and so it merited little of my attention.

What could be more important than a life dedicated to God?

IT WAS A WARM JULY EVENING WHEN I MET MY DEVIL AGAIN.

We were on a rooftop in Manhattan, the verdant scar of Central Park to one side, a nest of skyscrapers everywhere else. I was playing two parts in my black silk gown tonight: the dutiful daughter on her father's arm, looking lovely and gracious and expensive, and more invisibly, that of my uncle's little mouse, gathering whatever crumbs I could find. So far from Rome, so removed from the world of ecclesiastical politics, it was hard to imagine that I'd hear anything relevant to him, and yet my uncle was always interested in what I'd acquired, even if it was only the party talk of bankers and businessmen.

It's like panning for gold, he'd told me more than once before. *Sometimes you have to sift through a whole river of silt.*

At some point, my father and I danced, much to the

delight of the crowd. We played the role well, of doting father and loving daughter, of a family buffeted by grief but still holding steadfast to one another, and it only added to the venerable reputation of Laurence Bank. Other banks were conglomerates, were faceless entities with no soul, but here was Geoffrey Laurence, handsome and silvered at the temples looking fondly at his daughter; here was Geoffrey Laurence putting his only child first, above all else. A Laurence would be loyal, steady, about values and tradition. You could trust a Laurence with your money, our little performance said. You could trust a Laurence with your life.

It was, of course, only a performance. My father was warm to me when people were watching, and no other time, and I was privately repulsed by Laurence Bank.

You cannot serve both God and money, we are told. And I didn't intend to.

When we finished dancing, I felt someone approach. I knew to turn gradually, to give the appearance of slow reflexes and even slower perception—a trick Mortimer had taught me when I was a girl.

Always give the people around you a reason to underestimate you. Do it the minute you meet them, if you can.

But even years of tutelage from Mortimer couldn't make me school my face when I turned. It was the stranger from the dojo.

And he was holding out his hand to me.

He wore a tux tonight, a dark, dark navy, and that giant watch again. His hair was styled back, and despite the shadow on his square jaw, he looked crisp and polished. His dark blue eyes glinted in a shade lighter than the night sky as he said, "May I have this dance?"

My father pushed me forward, so gently that it looked like a pat on the shoulder, but his meaning was unmistakable. "Go on," he said in a friendly, fatherly tone.

Not that I would have refused anyway. I had so many questions for this stranger, so many things about him I wanted to know. They frothed inside me like foam on the sea as I took his hand and he led me out to the dance floor, and I had to consciously remember everything my uncle had taught me about finding answers, about sifting through people so subtly that they wouldn't know you'd been sifting at all.

The band began a song, some slow old standard, and we faced each other, my hand in his larger one, his other coming to rest against the bare skin of my back. My gown was fairly conservative—bankers didn't dress provocatively or with any kind of flash—but its one concession to sensuality was its back, which dropped all the way to the bottom of my spine.

I put my hand on his shoulder, which was just as firm and broad as it had looked under his tuxedo jacket, and we began to dance, moving effortlessly across the floor.

But when I looked up and met his eyes, I saw nothing of the polite man asking me to dance, nothing even of the unreadable stranger with a fake knife in his hand, ready to pin me to the floor.

He was looking at me with an expression so intense that I nearly recoiled in his arms. His mouth—fuller than I remembered, although I hadn't made up how strikingly shaped it was—was set in a sharp line, and his dark eyes glittered in a way that made alarm flare up my spine. It took every bit of my control not to react to his change in demeanor.

"Isolde Laurence," he said softly. "At last we meet for real."

"I'm sorry," I said carefully. "I think you have the better of me, Mister…?"

"Mark Trevena." He moved us easily in the dance, leading our steps with such surety and grace that I could almost forget that there were steps at all.

"Do you know my father, sir?"

There was the slightest hitch in his movement just then, barely noticeable to anyone else. I doubt even another dance partner would have noticed it. But I felt it like an earthquake.

My question had surprised him, maybe?

"In a manner of speaking," he said. "We're business associates. When the business is mutually beneficial."

His words were clipped, short. They betrayed nothing, which was something in and of itself. Actual business associates rarely had to be so cryptic.

Sometimes, both in sparring and in diplomacy, you had to stop dancing around your opponent and attack. I decided to take a more direct approach, just to see how he parried. "You don't have to dance with me, you know. If you don't want to."

There was no hitch in his movement this time, but the faintest curl of amusement pulled at the corner of his mouth. "Who's to say I'm not enjoying it?"

Our gazes locked. He was tall enough that I had to lift my chin to look at his face, and his strength was undeniable around me. I suddenly felt the yawn of years between us. Before now, my youth had been an asset, the way I moved through spaces as Mortimer's eyes and ears, but for the first time, I felt it like a liability.

This man, so much older than me, could outplay me, outmaneuver me. He could even kill me, if he chose—that he'd made clear enough in the dojo all those months ago.

I didn't think he wanted to kill me. But something about dancing with him under the night sky felt like dancing right into a trap that even I might not be able to escape from.

But then why did my chest feel so tight? Why did it feel like the air was falling, falling, right out of my lungs, as if it was suddenly made of something heavier than air, like iron or lead? Why was there was nothing left to keep my pulse moving normally?

And as we moved around the floor, our eyes still tight on each other's, my blood was pooling in all the wrong places. A flush on my cheeks and chest. Thick and hot in the bottom-most part of my belly. All from this man's cold, perceptive stare.

I hated it.

The music ended, proof if I ever needed it that God was watching over me, and I managed not to yank myself away from the tuxedoed danger, managed to wait for him to walk me attentively to the side of the dance floor, where my father stood talking to colleagues.

I still hadn't responded to his question about enjoying the dance, and before Mark released my hand from where he'd tucked it firmly in the crook of his elbow, he leaned in to murmur, "I took significant pleasure in our dance, Isolde. Worry not."

And then he straightened, smoothed his jacket, and with a jagged sort of smile, left me.

I felt the place where his hand had been on my back the rest of the night.

I WOKE AT DAWN THE NEXT DAY, MY HEART SLAMMING AGAINST my ribs, slick flesh pulsing between my legs. I wasn't ignorant of sex; I knew that I'd had an orgasm in my dream.

Just as I knew Mark Trevena had been in my dream.

I sat up and shivered on the edge of my bed, wanting —wanting—

My fingers twitched, my skin tingled. I imagined a knotted cord against my back, purging myself of unwanted lust, but my body was confused, too tangled from the dream, and the idea of whipping myself only stirred me more.

I shoved up from my bed and stumbled over to my

dresser. I would pray and then I'd run, and I'd run so far that even my own dreams were left behind me.

Two hours and five miles later, a chipper Bryn came up beside me. It was already hot, even this early in the morning, and the trees lining the Riverside Park path weren't enough to stop the pink flush under Bryn's light bronze cheeks.

"I heard you met our Knife Guy last night," she said by way of hello, matching my pace perfectly. "Lav told me."

Lavender was Bryn's older sister. Both Bryn's mother and father worked at Laurence Bank; Lav was engaged to a vice president of global markets there. Bryn's life was practically more involved with Laurence Bank than my own.

"His name is Mark Trevena. We danced." I didn't know why I added that last part. It didn't matter.

Who's to say I'm not enjoying it?

"Do you know what he does?" Bryn asked, looking over at me. Her dark ponytail swung in a long arc over her shoulders. She asked like she already knew, like the answer mattered.

"He said he was a business associate of my father's."

"Izzy, he runs a sex club."

I stumbled, barely catching myself before I fell. Of all the things she could have said, I would have never—

Sex clubs were real? Truly real?

"Lav said it's very secret, someplace in DC. And everyone goes there, like everyone who matters, and from all over the world. And it's not just a sex club, but it's like a fetish club or something. You know, spanking and people pretending to be puppies and stuff."

"A sex club," I repeated faintly. Our footfalls were back in sync now as we ran, but I felt like I could trip again at any moment. I'd never even been kissed, but I hadn't considered myself innocent, by any means. Half the morsels of information I brought back to Mortimer were in some way related to sex—who was having an affair, who wanted to be having an affair, and so forth, and so I'd considered myself worldly when it came to matters of the flesh.

But I was realizing just then that I had a young person's understanding of sex, that my notions of it were smooth and shallow and unshaded.

A sex club. A fetish club.

His eyes had been so piercing, had missed nothing. And that same gaze fell over the people at this club of his. Maybe while they were naked. Maybe while they were fornicating.

I didn't know why it all made me feel so shaky, disturbed. It didn't matter.

It didn't matter.

"The real question is why he was at a Laurence Bank party to begin with," Bryn said. "Do you think sex club owners make investments?"

I came to a stop near a railing overlooking the river and laced my hands above my head to help me breathe. "I don't know," I said. My words were ragged; sweat dripped down my chin. "I don't know."

"You know who would know." Bryn gave me a look, and if I'd had any breath left in me, I would have sighed.

"Yeah."

But Uncle Mortimer, the man who knew everything and everyone, didn't answer my messages when I sent them.

> Do you know a man named Mark Trevena? He was at the Laurence Bank party last night.

I paused and then added:

> He came to the dojo once last fall too.

> He knew my name.

There was no response.

For a day and a half, there was no response, and I tried not to let it preoccupy me. My uncle was a busy man, and

Rome was a busy place, and as much as he loved crumbs, the work of his life was moving boulders. A stranger on a rooftop half a world away wouldn't be the first of his concerns.

But I couldn't stop thinking about Mark Trevena, about his club in DC. About the way he'd looked at me.

I disliked it, I decided. I was certain that was what I could call the tangle of confusion, fascination, and restlessness. *Dislike.*

And I wasn't naive. I knew very few banks did business with exclusively ethical people. I knew that money was king in my father's world.

But there was one thing more important to him than money, and that was reputation, and surely…surely my father didn't know what Mark Trevena actually did. Surely he wouldn't want Laurence Bank anywhere near even the *idea* of a sex club.

At dinner that night, I broached the subject, careful to wait until my father had finished his first glass of wine but before he started his second. Receptive but not so loose that he became dismissive. My father appreciated manners, and so I made sure to frame my question in the polite tones of dinner chat.

"Lavender Flores-King mentioned something to Bryn about a guest at the party last night. The one who danced with me?"

My father, who'd been in the middle of cutting a piece of chicken, stopped. Looked up at me. "Mark Trevena," he said flatly.

"Yes."

His fingers tightened on his fork and knife for an instant. I saw how he made them relax before he resumed cutting his meat. "And what is it that Ms. Flores-King said?"

I summoned up my dislike, my instinctive disgust, the residual fear left behind by Mark Trevena's cutting stare, but I still kept my voice polite. "That Mark Trevena owns a sex club. A fetish club."

"Ah," my father said. "Is that all?"

Wasn't that enough? "I thought we were doing our utmost to keep Laurence Bank's image pristine. It would be one thing to take his money, but to allow him at our events? Allow him to dance with me?"

"Do you find what he does offensive?"

I stared at him. "Don't you? My entire life—and especially since Mum died—all I've heard is how appearances matter, how we must be above reproach always. It's what sets us apart from other banks. It's why people trust us."

My father's gaze when he leveled it at me was intractable. "People trust us because we take care of their money, Isolde. There are certain necessary evils that come with that responsibility. Necessary evils that we must allow as a family."

"But why should we? We're called to be upright, to be salt of the world—"

"Save me your moralistic bullshit, Isolde. You are *a child*, and you have no idea what you're talking about."

I was utterly stunned. My father might have been cool, he might have been distant and painfully exacting with my academic and social performances, but he never, *ever* spoke to me like that. And he *definitely* never would have before my mother died.

My father set down his fork and poured himself a full glass of wine, nearly to the brim. And then he drank the whole thing as if it were water.

I watched as he set the glass down a little too hard and then wiped his mouth with his napkin. "I didn't want to have this conversation yet, but it's just as well," he said shortly. "It was no accident that you met Mark Trevena last night. You will be seeing much more of him over the coming months—and years."

There was something in his tone—in his face—that made

my skin prickle, my muscles tense. Danger. After years and years in the dojo, my body often recognized danger before my mind could catch up.

"I will?" I asked, unable to modulate the wariness in my voice.

"Yes," my father said. "Because you are to marry him."

four

I laughed. I actually laughed.

Because it was laughable. Because it was absurd.

Because it was the exact opposite of everything I wanted.

But my father didn't laugh. He didn't even smile. Instead, he poured himself another glass of wine and drank from it slowly, his eyes somewhere in the middle distance.

I stopped laughing. "You aren't serious."

"I suggest you accustom yourself to the idea," he said tightly. "Because I am very serious."

He was, I could see it all over him. As serious as he'd been about my grades, about me going to university. And an unpleasant feeling bloomed deep in the pit of my stomach. "Is this why you wouldn't listen when I told you I wanted to take vows? Because you wanted me to marry some...some sex club owner? *Why*?"

"You are not taking any kind of vows, and I'm sick to death of hearing about it," my father bit out. "I could kill Mortimer for filling your head with that nonsense. You are my only heir, the sole container in which all of my work and my father's work and his father's work before him will pour into, and it was never a question that you would carry on the bank in my stead once I retire. You can hardly do that with a vow of poverty, Isolde. You can hardly do anything interesting with your life if you choose to spend it mumbling prayers and scurrying about doing your uncle's pointless little errands for a pointless, dying institution."

Small trembles had accumulated under my skin. I knew my father didn't want me to become a nun; I knew that as well as I knew his middle name or his birthday. But he'd never openly mocked me, never made my dreams sound stupid or gullible or small.

"It's what I want to do," I said, my nose stinging. I hated that I was so close to crying right now. I wanted to face my father with all my dignity armored around me, with logic and collectedness on my side. "It's what I am called to do."

"You are called *to be my daughter!*" my father roared suddenly, slamming his fist onto the table and making all the dishes jump. "You are called to obey *me*; you are called to heed *me*. And now I am telling you that you will marry Mark Trevena, and you will obey!"

"I will not," I said and got to my feet. My voice was quivering, but I would not falter, I would not give in. Like Catherine of Siena, I knew my own destiny. "I'm eighteen. You can't make me do anything I don't want to do. You can cut me off from all your money, and I will thank you for making my vow of poverty even easier to take. You can kick me out, but I've already inherited Cashel House in Ireland, and I'll go live there instead until I can find a monastery that will take me. There's nothing you hold over me that can make me do this."

I turned and left the room, my flats making a steady, even noise on the parquet wood of the penthouse floor.

I would not hurry or run. I wouldn't give him the satisfaction.

IT WAS NEAR MIDNIGHT WHEN I HEARD THE KNOCK AT MY door. It was a reluctant kind of sound—a tap instead of a rap —and it was only that small concession that made me say, "Come in."

My father stepped in, his tie unknotted, his jacket off. His hair, normally aggressively smoothed, was sticking up at the top, as if he'd been running his fingers through it. The whites of his eyes were bloodshot. I suspected he'd been drinking this entire time.

He dropped himself in the chair by my desk. Though our penthouse was generous in its living space—by Manhattan standards, anyway—my room wasn't spacious by any means. My father was close enough for me to smell his wine and sweat from where I sat against my headboard.

Father's gaze found the picture on the edge of my desk— him, me, and Mum, smiling together at Disney World. We were all slightly sunburned and giddy with sugar, and behind us were balloons and castle spires and an unrelenting subtropical sky. I remembered knowing I was too old to do something like fall asleep on my mother's shoulder during the Hall of Presidents show and doing it anyway, right in the middle of President Penley Luther's speech. I remembered how it had felt to walk between them, all of us linking hands. I remembered thinking I had the best family in the world.

Three weeks after that, my mother had died in a car crash.

Father touched the edge of the picture frame lightly, hesitantly, and then pulled his hand back.

"She wouldn't want me to do this either, you know," I said. My voice had lost its quaver—it was cold and clear.

But my father surprised me. "I know," he said, and then

27

he sighed. "I know that better than anyone. But her death changed more than her not being here, Isolde, and I think it's time you knew how much."

"Changed what? Us? The bank?"

"We have to think about the future differently. We have to think about this family differently, ensure our survival in more creative ways. Did Ms. Flores-King tell you what Mark Trevena used to do?"

"You mean before the sex club?" My voice had a bite to it that I rarely allowed, but my father seemed to expect it.

"Trevena was CIA. Special operations." My father paused, seemed to decide on a different way to start. "His club, Lyonesse, is different from its competitors in many ways, but the chief difference is this: he doesn't accept payment in money, only in information. His patrons are politicians, diplomats, celebrities, royalty. All of them have to pay in knowledge exclusive to their positions."

I absorbed this.

"So in a way, Mark has never left the field of intelligence," my father continued. "And *intelligence* is a generous word for what he used to do, anyway—he was the devil they sent in to scourge the other devils. And he was the best in the world at it."

I knew immediately what the appeal was for my father without being told. "So he knows things. Things you think could help the bank."

"He knows things. He knows people."

I looked down at my hands. "And that knowledge is worth me. My future."

"Your future is Laurence Bank, Isolde, and united with Mark Trevena's hoard of information…there is nothing the bank couldn't do. No place we couldn't reach, no person we couldn't sway. We would be unstoppable."

I didn't respond.

"This request isn't arbitrary," my father said as he came to his feet. "It's not meant to be cruel or to torment you or whatever else your teenage mind is telling you right now. It is the best step toward your future and the bank's that I can take."

I hated him just then. I hated that he was taking my reaction and making it seem as if I were the unreasonable one, the foolish one for having a plan for my life that didn't include him abruptly announcing that I was going to marry a stranger.

"I'm not doing it," I told him. My voice was shaking again, and it made me even more upset. "And you can't make me. You certainly can't convince me that this is the best thing for my future when I've already pledged it to God."

He didn't bother arguing with me; he must have known he'd get nowhere.

"Good night, Isolde."

I AVOIDED HIM FOR THE NEXT WEEK. WHICH WASN'T THAT difficult; though he made a point to eat dinner with me whenever he was in the same city as I was, he traveled enough that those dinners were very infrequent. After that, it was only a matter of spending as much time at the dojo as possible—hardly a sacrifice when I loved being there anyway.

I was running through my forms when the bell above the door rang. I turned, expecting to see another student or a delivery person, and then felt a boost of happiness when I saw my uncle standing there instead, grinning his gap-toothed grin, his pectoral cross and the gold ring on his finger winking in the cheap, flickering lights. He wore his black simar as always, red skullcap tucked tightly against his head.

"Mortimer!" I said and jogged over to give him a hug.

He patted my back fondly. "I had the feeling my favorite niece needed me. So here I am."

I pulled back and studied his face, which was pointless, since Mortimer's face never revealed anything he didn't want it to.

"Did Father tell you? About what he wants me to do?"

"Yes," Mortimer allowed with a sigh. He looked around the dojo and then back to the door. "Let's take a walk, you and I. Let me hear how you're feeling."

There were only two cities in the world where Mortimer could walk in his simar and skullcap and no one would bat an eye: New York City and Rome. And so we were completely ignored as we walked to the High Line and climbed its stairs, me in my gi and Mortimer in his cardinal vestments, our heads bent together as I told him everything that had happened.

"And then," I finished as we reached the path and started walking, "I told him that he couldn't make me do it. I'm eighteen, I don't need his money. My future was already in consecrated poverty, anyway."

The sun was bright and hot up here, and the lush greenery lining the path only added to the cloying humidity. Below us, I could see the creep and crawl of traffic, not so bad today, but still constant, incessant. Like blood through the city's veins.

Mortimer hadn't spoken yet, so I turned to look at him. I expected indignation on his face, maybe even disgust at my father's archaic thinking.

But instead, he looked pensive.

"What?" I asked, suddenly wary.

Mortimer's hands were laced behind his back, as they often were, and he had to turn his shoulders to look at me.

"I think you should do it," he said.

Something gaped and yawned inside my chest, an empty space absent of air or blood or anything. He could have slapped me across the face and I would have been less surprised.

"You think I should do it," I echoed. I stopped walking, feeling my pulse in my neck and my wrists, a pulse that still came even while breathing barely felt possible. "You think I should marry a stranger. For a bank."

My uncle stopped too, the simar swishing around his ankles as he took a step closer to me. It was a weekday and scorching to boot, and so the High Line was empty in both directions. It was just us and the plants bobbing in the concrete-scented breeze.

He stared at me, and I knew he was waiting for me to have an outburst, to plead my case, and I hated that I couldn't stop myself from speaking, from exploding. It was the exact lack of control that he had tried to tutor me against, but how could I stop myself? When he didn't seem to understand the situation at all?

"I want to be a nun," I said, my jaw tight to keep my voice from wavering. "I want to take vows. I can't do that if I marry this man. This man whom, I cannot stress enough, I don't know and whom I don't want to marry. I'm not a stock to be traded, I'm not an asset to be invested, and I'm not giving up my future to further my father's earthly glory." I was proud that I hadn't started crying yet, but I didn't know how much longer I could last. I was gutted. Worse than gutted, because it felt like he'd ripped my soul out along with my viscera and flung it all over the railing to the street below.

And that was before I realized something even worse.

"You *knew*," I choked out. "At Christmastime, this is what Father was talking to you about. You knew this was coming, and you let me believe..."

I will never steer you away from what God needs you to do.

Why hadn't I paid attention to how vague his assurances had been then? Why hadn't I dug deeper, insisted on more?

Mortimer arched an eyebrow at me in sympathy. "My

child, I hear you, and I see the betrayal in your face. Will you let me explain? Let me make my case?"

"What case is there to make?" My voice was quiet now, almost more exhalation than speech. "I want to be a nun. I've wanted it since I was twelve. I want to serve you and the Church and God, and I cannot do any of that if I am married."

"I sometimes forget," Mortimer replied softly, "how very young you are. You have the faith and commitment of someone much older, but you still think so categorically, so broadly. In unqualified absolutes."

I bristled and he patted the air in a quelling gesture.

"I don't mean that in deprecatory way, Isolde, it's only the truth. You are eighteen, and there are things that you will view with an eighteen-year-old's eyes. I've sharpened you into a blade, but being sharp is only half a blade's job. The other half is knowing when and where to cut. I will teach you that too, I promise."

I stared at him. "If I married Mark, which I won't, you couldn't promise me any such thing. I won't be able to take vows. I won't be able to work for you or the Church."

Mortimer's mouth tilted up in a fond smile. "Come," he said, wandering over to the railing and leaning against it. The simar blew a little in the breeze as I joined him, and I thought about the habit I wouldn't be able to wear if I listened to him and my father.

I braced my forearms on the railing and made a point not to look at him. Childish maybe, but he and the sisters were the ones who had taught me to fight with every weapon I had.

"Now, the issue of your vocation. I am disappointed you did not see the solution to this on your own, Isolde, but I suppose I've failed you in teaching you to think outside convention. You, of course, can take your vows and don your habit after your marriage to Mark Trevena is concluded."

I gave a sharp laugh. "How am I supposed to *conclude* a marriage when divorce is forbidden?"

"An annulment," my uncle said smoothly. "Once the marriage is annulled, you will be free to pursue any vocation you like. Any future you like."

"Annulments are only for unconsummated marriages." It was so strange to be talking about this with my uncle of all people, but he clearly wasn't understanding the stakes. "Do you think the owner of a sex club will allow for an unconsummated marriage?"

"Do you think the Church will not allow for whatever I arrange for you? I'd be able to claim that you were not fully consenting; I can claim Pauline privilege if Mark's baptism records are conveniently lost—but more importantly, I have made myself indispensable to the Holy Father. If my niece needs a marriage to *conclude*, I will see it done, no matter if you shared his bed or not. The truth is a fuzzy thing when we need it to be."

I did turn to look at him then, my fingers gripping the railing. I felt like the ground was tilting under my feet, but so slightly that only I could feel it. "That would be lying," I said faintly. "Non loqueris falsum testimonium. You shall not bear false witness."

"Is it false witness, Isolde? Truly? The fact of what might happen between your body and Mark Trevena's is not the same as the holy truth; your sacrifice will make inviolable the reality of your spiritual chastity."

"My *sacrifice*."

"Yes," my uncle said earnestly. "Because I have not explained to you yet—of course you wouldn't see yet—how powerful this alliance could be."

"I already know—"

"No, my child, you don't. You know what your father has told you, that he wants access to Mark's hoard of information to help his ridiculous bank. I don't care about your father

33

making more money he doesn't need. But the information you could find for me and Rome—to help keep the faithful safe—Isolde, the work that you could do in a moment, that I couldn't do in a lifetime…"

But it wouldn't be the work of a moment, why couldn't he understand this? It would be days and weeks and years and maybe the rest of my life, and those days and weeks would feel like eternities with Mark Trevena. I thought of his cold, searching gaze at the rooftop party, of his relentless mastery in the dojo that day, when he had taken me down to the mats over and over again. It would be torture. And that was even subtracting the effort of trying to get whatever information my father and Mortimer wanted so dearly.

"All that to say," Mortimer continued, "the Church will not hold this powerful victory against you. You will be rewarded, handsomely. Your heart's desire for this temporary sacrifice."

"This word again," I murmured. "Sacrifice. This is not a sacrifice. This is a violation of God's will."

"You say this with a confidence you cannot have." My uncle shook his head, smiling at me. "Who better to know God's will than me? This is not a waste, like Jephthah with his daughter, but rather a gift from God. You will be serving me and the Church even more thoroughly than you and I had planned. You will be proximate to all the information, and all the people, I would ever send you to find, and instead of you having to sift for gold, it would be poured into your waiting hands."

He lifted a hand to my shoulder, the same steady, reassuring hand that had guided me all my life. The hand that had kept me steady through my mother's funeral, steady when I couldn't stop crying, steady when my father was so sick of my hysterics that he didn't even want me at the service. My uncle had insisted, had folded me under his arm, his black cape covering me.

Her tears are holy, he'd said to my father. *To hide her tears is to hide God's love for Inis today*. He'd comforted me, prayed with me. Told me that God was inside my pain because God had also lost someone he loved, his one begotten son, and only God was big enough, gentle and patient enough, to receive all the pain and emptiness I'd felt and to fold it inside of his mighty heart.

My uncle had enrolled me in karate, had given me Ignatius of Loyola and Thomas Aquinas to read, stacked alongside *The Prince* and *Leviathan* and *The Book of Five Rings*. He'd given me *The Art of War* and Marcus Aurelius's *Meditations* in leather-bound editions small enough to fit in my schoolbags; he'd listened to me attentively when I'd told him what I'd thought of them.

The hand that he lifted to my shoulder now was a hand more responsible for who I was today than my father's own hand—or even my mother's.

His cardinal's ring was a glittering gold beacon in the sunlight.

"We talk often of lifting our pain and suffering up to God," he said. "What greater pain than this? What greater suffering than this? You would be offering up so much more than a wish, Isolde, but a *calling*. You would be offering to Heaven a jewel so rare that few can even imagine it. Not just an act or a desire, but an entire life. Like Christ, you are laying down your very future."

I wavered.

Looking into his eyes, blue at the edges, green in the center, the two of them slightly different in their mottling, I couldn't see anyone but the man who'd raised me. The man who'd given me a person to be when everything seemed dead and buried along with Inis Laurence.

That Isolde trusted him implicitly. *That* Isolde wanted nothing more than to help him build the kingdom of God here on Earth.

35

And here he was saying that I needed to do it another way than the way we'd planned.

"But I can't," I said. Faintly. "I can't marry someone I don't know…"

"For God," my uncle said, "you can do anything. All things are possible through him."

"But what if…" I couldn't finish the question. Not to my uncle. But what if I had to have sex with Mark? Visit his sex club? A marriage *ceremony* was one thing, but what did being the wife of Mark Trevena actually entail?

Was any information worth that price?

Mortimer gave me a sad smile. "Are you afraid you aren't strong enough?"

Strong enough? I ran and sparred and punched bags until my shoulders gave out; each night before bed, I spent ten minutes kicking a wooden post covered with old tires to strengthen my shins. I had straight As and an immaculate school career despite my heart already belonging to my future vocation; I had managed to survive six years without Inis Laurence.

"I know I'm strong enough," I said with a sharp lift of my chin, and it was only as Mortimer's eyes flickered with triumph that I realized I'd taken his bait.

"Then this is only a test," he said. "A test you shall pass with flying colors."

I looked away, my entire body at war with itself. There were so many saints who'd asked for tests, who'd begged for them. Begged for any kind of suffering they could bear on behalf of the world. That was what you did if you were holy. You suffered and then offered that pain up to God to help sanctify souls in purgatory, for the salvation of souls here on Earth.

To suffer was to be holy.

"I will be here to guide you," my uncle said, squeezing my

shoulder now. "To keep you safe. And the moment you need the marriage over, I will see it done."

"I might be afraid," I finally admitted. "Of Mark. Of never finding my way out of this marriage."

"Even Christ was afraid in Gethsemane. But the Father guided the Son to his purpose, and so shall I with you. In fact…"

He dropped his hand from my shoulder as I looked back at him. Hopelessness was a weight on my chest, but perhaps that was my selfishness talking, my fear. I should be offering that hopelessness up to God.

He seemed to be considering something, and then nodded to himself, that eternal eyebrow arched. "Yes," he said after a long moment. "You're ready. You're ready to visit Rome and begin working for me properly soon. Then I think you'll see what a benediction God has brought us in the shape of Mark Trevena."

five

Three weeks later, and I was climbing out of a black car in front of a Midtown skyscraper, trying to quell the nervousness that kept crawling under my skin.

When my father had informed me that Mark Trevena wanted to have dinner with me, alone, I'd almost refused.

But then I'd relented. What was the point in refusing? I'd agreed to marry him; negotiations between him and my father were nearly finished. It felt childish to deny him dinner if I was already conceding my future, my life, my soul.

I would be resolute. I would be courageous.

I would make Marcus Aurelius and Jesus proud of me.

I wore a silk pewter blue dress, tea length and long-sleeved, with a lapeled neckline that revealed nothing more than my clavicle. I'd worn minimal makeup and had pulled my hair into a sleek ponytail.

As if by dressing simply enough, I could pretend to him and myself that I hadn't been having arching, twisting dreams for the last three weeks—dreams that featured cold blue eyes and large, capable hands.

It meant nothing. It meant only that lust was nipping at my heels like any other temptation, but I would beat it back.

Yes, I was marrying Mark for the uncle and Church I loved, but no one could make me *want* to. That I would keep for myself.

A doorman greeted me and escorted me to the elevator that would take me to the restaurant, and I stepped inside. My father had said that Mark wanted to discuss certain things separately with me—what, I wasn't sure, given that so much had already been resolved. The wedding wouldn't take place until I graduated from Columbia, so I had at least four years to brace myself. There would be a prenup, ironclad, to protect the Laurence fortune and Mark's own assets. We would split our time between his house in DC and his other properties in Manhattan, Maine, and England. He would not interfere with my having a career.

We would have a Catholic wedding.

To my mind, there was little else to discuss. Ideally we wouldn't need to see each other until the wedding ceremony itself. Four years from now…

So much could happen in four years.

The elevator lifted, lifting my stomach, and then came to a crisp stop. I gave myself one instant to rub my fingers against my palms, one instant to take a deep inhale, and then by the time the elevator doors opened, I knew I appeared contained and cool. Unfazed by meeting with my fourteen-years-older fiancé.

A maître d' greeted me as I stepped out of the elevator.

"Miss Laurence," he said with a small bow. "Your party is waiting for you. Right this way."

I followed him, although there would have been no need. Even though it was a Friday evening, the restaurant was completely and utterly empty, save for one guest, seated at a table by the window.

Beyond him was the blue and pink gloaming of Manhattan twilight, interrupted with dark spires and glowing windows. I could see his profile against it, a strong nose and sculpted lips, hair styled back away from his face. It was cut shorter on the sides, disguising nothing of those brutally high cheekbones and that carved jaw. He wore a suit like most people wore nothing, like it was the most natural thing in the world to be in wool so finely tailored that it hugged his shoulder and arm as he lifted a glass of something clear to his lips and drank.

I would not swallow. I would not pay attention to the pulse beating in my neck. But I could admit privately that I had forgotten how handsome he was, had forgotten the way he filled a space just by being in it. And when he turned those dark eyes on me, I also had to admit something worse.

His attention affected me.

Deeply.

No one had ever looked at me like Mark Trevena had the night of the party, like he was right now. Like he wanted to cut me open and taste the blood that came out, and then make me taste it too.

Like it wouldn't be enough to see my secrets...he would want to consume them.

It was cold and horrible—horrible because every time he looked at me, I felt the opposite of cold. I felt something that could almost be called anger, but it wasn't like any anger I'd ever felt before.

Mark stood with a dip of his head and then pulled out my chair before the maître d' could do it for me. He waited for me to sit before pushing my chair in and then taking his own seat and reaching for his glass. Everything was done with impeccable manners, hypnotic grace. I thought again of him in the dojo that day, holding the knife, walking so smoothly, so casually...right until he'd pounced.

It struck me that this might be the same. There weren't knives, no one would be pinned literally to the floor, but why would he need to resort to such obvious measures when he already had me cornered so effectively?

Saint Michael the Archangel, defend us in battle, I prayed silently as I set my clutch next to me on the seat and met Mark's cool, appraising gaze. *Be our protection against the wickedness and snares of the devil.*

"Thank you for meeting me," Mark said after a moment. His voice was as cool as his gaze. "I wasn't sure if you would come."

I hadn't been sure if I would come either, but I supposed I wasn't wired for half sacrifices. If I was going to do this, then I needed to do it. Truly and wholly, sparing nothing. Offering everything up to God.

"It seemed smart," I replied. "It will be good for us to establish rapport over the next four years."

"Rapport," said Mark. "Yes, I agree."

I looked around at the sea of empty tables, lit by gentle ambient light and the lights of the city beyond. "It's quiet for a Friday night."

"Yes, I made sure it would be," Mark said, and then, "Ah, thank you," as the waiter presented us with heavy, leather-mounted menus.

Made sure?

I stared at him over my menu. "You reserved the entire restaurant?" I was no stranger to money, but Laurences weren't flashy with their wealth. Bankers needed to appear trustworthy and careful above all else. Better to buy property, to expand into CDs or bonds, than to use wealth in some gauche display.

Although I wasn't sure I could use the word *gauche* for Mark. He didn't seem smug or sleazy as he met my eyes with his brows lifted. He seemed as aloof as ever, like he didn't care if I was impressed or disgusted by such a waste of money.

"We have things to discuss that I preferred not to have an audience for," he said, and then glanced down at his menu. "This seemed like the most elegant solution."

I didn't know if I could agree with that, but perhaps the alternatives weren't any better. It wasn't as if I would have felt comfortable going to wherever he lived. And perhaps he felt the same way about being in my father's house.

At least this was neutral ground.

We each ordered—me the lobster and him the wagyu beef—the waiter took our menus, and then we were left completely alone.

He didn't speak first, and I decided to take the field, like a white pawn in a chess game. "My father said you had things you wanted to negotiate tonight."

"Yes," he said, and then his eyes moved over my face. His expression flickered with displeasure, his lips twisting together. "What's that?"

"What?"

He reached across the table and brushed his fingertips against the hairline near my temple. I flinched; firstly, because he'd touched me, and secondly, because there was a deep bruise there.

"Oh," I said, lightly rubbing a knuckle against the spot. "Sister Mary Alice hit me in the head with a bo staff."

"I hope you appreciate how unique that sentence is."

I lifted a shoulder.

My reaction seemed to amuse him, because the corner of his mouth pressed in before he folded his long-fingered hands on the table and leveled a stare at me. "I'd like for us to speak transparently tonight. You know what I do," he said without further preamble. "You know about the club."

I hadn't expected him to be so direct about it, although I wasn't sure *why* I'd thought that, only that it had seemed too tawdry to address in public. Or at all.

"Yes," I said after a beat. "I know about it."

"What do you know?" asked Mark.

"That it's a club for sex." I knew my voice betrayed nothing, which was a relief, because I still felt everything about it. Everything about marrying into it.

"Yes. Among other things," he responded, and it dawned on me, very slowly, what should have been obvious from the beginning. Mark didn't merely demand information as an admittance fee; the club was a source of information all on its own. It must have been like the Vatican in that way—you gathered enough powerful people in one place, a place where they felt private and privileged, and the information flowed with no outside incentive. Even just watching his guests interact would be valuable… and if Mortimer had been interested in who pulled whom aside for a chat in a ballroom corner, how much more would he want to know who spent time together at a sex club?

"…to the central issue, which is that I'm very involved with the running of my club, and I'm very visible there," Mark was saying. I forced my attention back to his cool, polite voice. "Unfortunately, I don't think anyone will believe that I would marry someone who wasn't also part of my world."

My stomach lifted once, and then dropped. I didn't want to be right about where this was going.

"I understand you've agreed to this marriage because it will help your father's bank." Mark's voice was devoid of any judgement; if he thought that was a callow or greedy reason, he didn't show it. I was relieved he was unaware of my uncle's role in my life, and of his requests. It was infinitely safer and easier if Mark believed helping my father's company was the only reason I was doing this.

It made me wonder about his reasons. Why marry someone so young, so outside his world? Why marry someone he didn't know? Surely his sex club was filled with more appetizing prospects than me.

"Why did *you* agree?" I asked him. "What was in it for you?"

Mark's expression remained a cipher, but his finger trailed

along the rim of his glass. The ice in his drink had long ago melted, and I wondered what was inside. Gin? Vodka?

"Information can flow both ways," he answered finally. "Laurence Bank has some very powerful clients. Both clients that it shares with me, and clients that are of interest to *my* clients. Access to what your father knows about these people would be extremely beneficial to me."

So it boiled down to the same thing for Mark and my father and Mortimer too. I was a means to an end, and that end was the mysterious, all-important *information*. Mortimer wanted it for the Church, my father for money.

I didn't know why Mark wanted it. Perhaps only to broker it, to profit from it. To consolidate his obscure throne back in DC.

Information.

I should have been relieved that was all Mark wanted. I wondered why I was abruptly upset instead. I rolled my lips together and looked down at the table. Mark's hand on his glass was at the very corner of my vision, and I watched as his finger stopped moving along the edge. As it lifted, and then he rubbed his thumb over the knuckle once before resting his hand on the table.

"That's not the entire truth," he said. There was something a little rougher in his voice now, like he was admitting something he wasn't sure he should. "It's part of the truth, certainly, but not the whole."

I lifted my eyes from his hand to his face. "What is the whole?"

A beat passed. To anyone else, it would have been nothing more than a second. But to two people like us, used to slicing and stabbing and all the other things that could happen in the blink of an eye, the beat felt like an hour. Like a year.

"I asked for you," he said.

My heart jerked in my chest. My face burned.

"You asked for me? Why?" The words were faint on my lips.

He regarded me. "Because I wanted you," he said, like it was that simple.

I didn't know what to say to that. I didn't even know what to think...except that I had been foolish to be disappointed by Mark only wanting access to information from our marriage.

This was worse. This was much worse.

"But I'm aware that to you, this arrangement is transactional," Mark went on before I could gather my thoughts, "and so: tonight's dinner. Because there is a needle we must thread between you and me, if we want our relationship to appear genuine."

The waiter arrived with our food just then, and another glass of something clear on ice for Mark.

Genuine. I thought about the word as the waiter explained our plates to us, as I stared at my poached lobster with grape and fennel salad. I could tell Mark that our relationship appearing genuine meant very little to me. What did I care if other people knew our relationship was fake? And really, what did *he* care?

But no. I immediately saw the problem here; I saw why it mattered. The more natural our relationship appeared, the more leverage we both had for gathering information. The more I could ingratiate myself into Mark's world and gather crumbs for my uncle.

We needed to play the part.

"I run my club carefully," said Mark after the waiter left. "I run it so that both my authority and my reputation are unquestioned. Part of this is creating an armor of loyalty among those closest to me. If there is a perceived gap between me and my wife, then you could see how this armor would appear fissured. Ripe for exploiting."

I took up my knife and fork and began eating. "Does the owner of a sex club have that many enemies?"

A flicker around the edges of his mouth. "You'd be surprised."

The lobster was delicious, the salad bright on my tongue. Mark cut into his beef with the precision of a surgeon and the unconscious habit of a butcher. I watched as the blood-red meat made it to his lips. When he chewed, that startlingly perfect jaw flexed.

"So there shouldn't be any perceived gap between us," I said, ducking my eyes down to my plate before he could catch me staring at him as he ate.

"Yes, and here we come to the heart of the matter. Are you familiar with kink at all?"

There was something buzzing under my skin. A warning maybe. An ancient instinct that told me that a storm was coming, that a wolf was in the woods.

I could feel Mark's gaze on my face, and I fought the urge to look up at him. I studiously cut another piece of lobster and put it in my mouth.

When it became clear that he was not going to allow silence to be its own answer, I set down my fork and swallowed my food. After a drink of water, I said, more self-consciously than I wanted, "It's like…BDSM."

"Yes," he said, although the word was weighted with hesitation. Like there was more he wanted to add but was holding back for now. "For our purposes tonight, that's close enough."

The diligent student in me, eternally craving recognition and praise, cast around for more that I could say. Because I wasn't completely ignorant of BDSM—or kink, as Mark called it. There were movies, jokes. What Bryn had said during our run.

"And there are people dressing up," I said, making sure to paraphrase her comment about puppies more nicely. "And playing pretend."

"Roleplaying is certainly on the menu for those who want it."

46

"Is it…" I hesitated. "Is it on *your* menu?"

There was a graceful lift of his shoulder. "Let's say it's an aperitif worth having occasionally. Kink is expansive; it is so much more than any one thing. But if you're asking about my tastes, then I can tell you that they typically distill into two things—power and sensation. One I like to have. The other I like to give."

I thought about this. "So when you say that there shouldn't be a gap between us…"

"If people are to believe that I've claimed you as my bride, then they will need to believe that you are currently my submissive."

Submissive?

My reaction to the word must have shown on my face, because one of his eyebrows quirked. "It is more complicated than what I believe you are thinking right now, but the most important piece of this is that I do not expect you to be my submissive in truth."

"You don't?"

"I like my play partners willing," Mark said. "A future bride I would want infinitely more so."

"I see," I said calmly, as if my heart weren't hammering against my ribs. "So what are you proposing then? To present this illusion?"

"That you *pretend* to be my submissive leading up to the wedding," he explained, as if it should have been obvious. "I think we can be strategic with how often we display our relationship at Lyonesse. If we choose our opportunities wisely, we can be very sparing indeed, especially with you attending Columbia."

There went my hopes of not seeing him until the wedding. Despair yanked at my stomach.

My cage was closing too fast.

"How would I pretend to be your submissive?" How *could*

one pretend such a thing? "I don't even really know what one is."

"A submissive is a person who likes to be on the receiving end of things like power and sensation, nothing more." He paused, as if deciding what to say next. "I like pleasure and pain, Isolde. It's easy enough to make a facsimile of both."

I tried to settle my pulse. I didn't even know why it was racing now. Mark didn't expect anything real from me... surely that was a relief. Surely I was satisfied by that. "Truly?"

"Much like sparring is to a real fight, we can present a convincing performance with a minimum of contact. Regretfully, however, I must tell you that there will almost certainly have to be *some* contact."

My fiancé didn't look regretful, though. His posture had straightened infinitesimally, and his eyes were even darker now, darker than they'd been all night.

I asked for you.

I wanted you.

"So you will pretend to give me pain?" I asked quietly.

"And pleasure."

"And pleasure?"

His fingers curled around his glass, almost unconsciously, but he didn't take a drink. "Some of it will have to be real, you understand. Performing submission will be very close to actually doing it. We will have to take the same precautions. You will have to learn the same rules."

I looked out at the city. There was still an endless buzzing under my skin. "Will we have sex?"

"Do you want to?"

I gave him a sharp look. "I wanted to be a nun before this."

Mark returned my gaze with his own cool one, as if to tell me that he found this to be an incomplete answer.

I opened my mouth to tell him that it wasn't incomplete at

all, that of course I didn't want to have sex. But the words wouldn't come.

I realized, with slow-dawning horror, that saying them would feel like lying.

"You do not have to have sex with me, Isolde, but I will say this—I am possessive by nature. Once we are married, I'm not interested in you having sex with anyone else, even if we aren't fucking. In addition to my...nature, it would not help our carefully crafted appearance of unity if an affair of yours became known."

As if I would tarnish such a hard-bought offering to God with a sin as cheap as adultery. "That won't be a problem." It was my turn to lift a brow. "Will it be a problem for you?"

Mark smiled. The first smile of the night.

It was terrifying.

"After we wed, I will be as faithful as you are," Mark said. "How does that sound?"

I couldn't tell if he was being transparent or something worse. "It sounds acceptable to me," I said guardedly.

The smile deepened the barest amount, before he turned serious again. "Issues of fidelity aside, we'll need to expand your idea of sex. It's far more than just penetration, and it's also a signature of my play. The people at my club know this about me." He spread his hands on the table, as if to say, *this is out of my control*. "Our play might be pretend at its core, but its appearance will need to be sexual to be believable to the people watching."

Yes, of course, people watching. That was what this entire conversation had been about. People would watch me and Mark together; they would watch me pretending to submit. It almost made me light-headed to think about, but in a way that reminded me of the first few seconds before a sparring match at a tournament. It was uncomfortably close to excitement.

49

"The sexual parts...will they be like sparring too? As pretend as we can make them?"

"As much as possible." Mark turned his head to gaze out at the city, revealing the brutal beauty of his profile. His full mouth curved in another smile. "Unless you ask me otherwise in the moment, however."

Which would never happen.

I followed his gaze out the window, seeing what he was seeing. A canyon of glass and steel and concrete, and beyond it, the darkness of water.

This is the bed you chose. The bed you agreed to climb into.

I could say no. I could refuse this and tell Mark he needed to find some other way to make us appear like a united front to his world.

Or I could stand up, go home, and tell my father that this whole farce of a marriage was off.

But I wasn't the girl who shied away. Not from punches, not from pushups, not from wringing hour after hour of training from my body. I wasn't the girl who ran away from what was difficult or even impossible.

If this was what was being asked of me, then I would excel at it. And perhaps I would win Mark's loyalty as well. Perhaps it would be as easy as a few quasi-sexual performances to get everything Mortimer wanted from Mark.

And the sooner Mortimer had what he wanted, the sooner I could end this marriage altogether.

Yes, this was the shortest, sharpest course of action.

"I'll do it," I said to the dark window.

"Wonderful," said my fiancé. "We'll start rehearsing tomorrow."

Rehearsing.

It made sense. I could hardly show up to Mark's club and expect to perform my new role flawlessly on the first try. Like learning how to use a knife or reciting a new prayer, mastery only came through practice, praxis.

So yes, rehearsing was necessary, yes, I'd do it, but there was a slender coil of horror in my chest as I nodded. Not the least because I'd hoped to be untouched by this arrangement until my wedding day…but also, there was a danger here. And *rehearsing* with Mark felt like inviting that danger to scent my naked and exposed throat.

"In the meantime…"

He took my left hand where it rested on the table and wrapped his fingers around it. The contact nearly made me jump; his hand was huge and warm and the strength restrained in it was unnerving. I still noticed when his other hand produced a ring, which flashed and gleamed as he slid it onto my finger.

"As long as we are playing the part," he murmured, moving the ring gently past my knuckles and to the base of my finger. When he finished, I held it up to stare at it. A cluster of rubies dotted the middle like ripe fruit, and the band was made of twisting gold, wrought like vines and leaves.

"Honeysuckle," Mark said softly. "My grandmother told me once that it was the symbol of a good marriage."

I stared at it, at the rubies that were dark in the low light of the restaurant, at the twisted vines. It was the most unusual ring I'd ever seen.

It was also the most beautiful.

"Thank you," I whispered. I didn't know what else to say, because it was slamming into me just then, in a way that all the plans and negotiations could never have done before.

I had a ring on my finger.

I was getting married.

"Tomorrow," Mark said, his voice twisted with promise. "We will begin."

six

We did not begin. Mark was called back to DC on business later that night and sent his regrets via text message.

In fact, he couldn't make it up to Manhattan for another eight weeks, which should have meant a glorious reprieve while I started attending Columbia, but only meant my nerves felt scraped raw every day I didn't hear from him. Would it be tonight that I would be summoned? Tomorrow? The day after that?

During classes, during karate, and during my morning and evening prayers. It was like being haunted, but this was no ghost from the past. This was my future, haunting me.

Mark did send me reading materials, however—a link to a digital folder attached to a short email.

Isolde, you may find these useful in supporting our charade. I will happily answer any questions you have.

Yours faithfully,
Mark Trevena

I opened the email while sitting in the cavernous reading room of one of Columbia's libraries. Chandeliers hung above me, and all around me were sighs and echoes and the soft flutter of turning pages. For a long moment, regret was an axe splitting me in half.

I could be just like everyone else in here, my biggest problem some upcoming paper, my highest stakes a GPA no one outside of the world of academia would ever care about. I could have the rest of my life unspooling in front of me, a beckoning road. I could have choices and possibilities and mistakes to make.

But I was spoken for, my future was spoken for, and instead of fretting over tests or thinking of cute classmates, I was worried about pretending to be a submissive for a fiancé I didn't want, all while trying to use said fiancé to help my father's bank so that I could *really* help my uncle protect the Church. It was a tangle of pretense that I already felt anchored and cinched by. Strangled by.

And it had barely even started.

I closed my eyes for a minute, pushing my fear and my anger back down into my stomach. I would make it through this. I had made it through every task that had ever been set to me; how could I fail when Mortimer had made sure I knew how important this was?

I opened my eyes, and making sure no one had a good sightline on my laptop, I clicked the link and began studying kink like it was a class I needed to graduate.

IT WAS THE FIRST TRULY COLD DAY OF THE SCHOOL YEAR WHEN Mark texted me.

> I'll be in the city next week. I presume the
> reading material was sufficient?

I paused as I read his message, the bracing wind seeking my skin through my scarf. Other students brushed past me as I stood on the plaza in the middle of campus; it was the beginning of December and the end-of-semester desperation had taken hold. I too had been mildly stressed about my final projects and exams, but Mark's text wiped that all away. There now was something much larger to preoccupy my thoughts.

> It was.

And then I almost laughed at the absurdity of it all. *Sufficient*. Like I'd been reading up on how to change a doorknob or make raspberry jam.

> I think I understand enough to play the part.

> You are a good student. I believe it.

I was a good student. I'd read every word of what he'd sent me, and I could be tested on it, quizzed, cross-examined. I now knew the theory of dominance and submission, the biological responses to pain, pleasure, and deprivation, and the different methods to administer each. I knew more about Mark's club now too—a glass citadel by the water named Lyonesse. It had just opened a couple of years ago, and was already famed for its exclusivity and utter, utter secrecy. People flew from around the world to go there.

So yes, I knew so much more than I had before. Facts, data. Explanations and history.

But I still couldn't reconcile the idea of myself with that word. *Submissive*.

I hated that I was grateful to Mark for allowing me this small reprieve of merely pretending submission, but I was, I was grateful.

And if there was a part of me that lingered over the idea of punishment, if there was a part of me that noticed how very close this was to corporal penance, that remembered dreams best forgotten…

Well. No one had to know but me and God.

> I can meet you tonight.

I typed it before I could lose my nerve. There was no point in delaying it—it had to happen, and the more practice I had, the better I'd be at pretending in front of other people. And it was stupid to be nervous about seeing Mark again.

He was my fiancé; he would be my husband. Seeing each other was inevitable. How much, I still wasn't sure, but I was bracing myself for anything.

And at some point, surely, his eyes had to grow warmer? His manner less cutting? I recognized I was hardly a cuddly person myself, but I did think I was easy to be around. Fair to the people around me.

Or maybe he was cool and detached with everyone? Perhaps he'd never been able to turn off whatever he'd needed to excel when he'd been in the CIA. *The devil they sent in to scourge the other devils.* That's what my father had said about him.

> I'll be looking forward to it.

He sent an address next, an expensive new-build on Billionaire's Row. His Manhattan residence, I assumed.

With a deep, steadying breath, I turned on my heel and started walking the way I'd come. I needed to get ready.

IF I'D NEEDED PROOF THAT WHATEVER MARK DID AT LYONESSE was profitable, here it was, because no one was buying a penthouse like this with a former government employee's salary.

When the elevator to his home opened, I was greeted by two stories of windows overlooking Central Park, a cavernous space of glass and white walls and orderly bookshelves. I stepped forward, noting that aside from one hallway behind me, everything else on both levels was open. It should have felt wasteful, this much space in Manhattan, but there was something so pragmatic about the way it was finished and furnished that it was hard to find fault with it. It wasn't trying to point to anything more—not money, not power, not pretension—and for that reason the wealth and power it represented felt all the more apparent.

"Isolde," came a voice from my left. I turned to see Mark walking toward me, wearing only slacks and a button-down shirt with the sleeves rolled up. His shoes gleamed against the dark wood floors.

His eyes went immediately to my left hand, and I thought I saw a flash of satisfaction in them when he saw that I was wearing his ring.

"I'm glad you could make it tonight," he said. He stopped just behind me, and I could feel, rather than see, that his hands had lifted. Awareness prickled at the back of my neck as adrenaline injected itself into my bloodstream. Was he going to grab me from behind? Reach around to crush my throat?

"May I?" he asked, in a voice that would have been gallant if it weren't so low and rough.

The coat. He wanted to help me with my coat.

"Yes," I said, and the word came out too faint, too weak. "Thank you."

"Manners. I like that." He deftly unwound my scarf and pulled it from my neck, and the pads of his fingers brushed against my throat. I prayed he didn't notice the tremble that went through me then—from fear, from leftover adrenaline. From the knowledge that tonight I would learn how to be *his*, even if it was only to act the part later.

He eased me out of my coat with a fluid grace that betrayed much practice, and then I heard footsteps. I turned to see him putting my things away in a neat little closet, and I took a moment to absorb Mark in his own domain while he was occupied.

He still moved like he did that day in the dojo with the knife, with a sort of casual grace—but there was something more languid about his movements here. I wouldn't call it *relaxed*, because purpose was still scrawled all over his actions, cut into the unreadable expression on his face. But there was something more patient about him, a patience that felt almost leisurely. A man who had all the time in the world to do what he wanted.

He closed the door to the coat closet and moved to face me. And all that purpose and patience was now bent on me. As if he was so secure here in his minimalist aerie that he could pour all of his attention on me instead of his surroundings.

My breath caught in my chest as his eyes dropped down my body. I hadn't known what to wear to a fake BDSM training session, so I'd worn high-waisted bike shorts and a sports bra; he'd be able to see the shape of my body, but very little else, save for a strip of skin between my bra and shorts. My breasts were nothing special and mostly contained by the bra, and the shorts came down nearly to my knees.

When I'd dressed, I'd imagined his ire being piqued by

this obvious barrier between him and my body, this clear signal that sex was nowhere on the table. I'd imagined him looking disappointed, maybe, or even pensive, like he was thinking of a way to get me out of my clothes.

I'd been wrong.

Mark nodded at me, and there was approval in his tone when he said, "Good. Follow me."

He led me to the glass-railed stairs in the corner, and I followed him up to the second floor of the penthouse, which was lofted above the first. The stairs were meant to capture the best of the view—the park, the lights, the dark ribbon of the river—but my eyes went to the man in front of me. The narrow hips, the wide shoulders stretching the seams of his shirt. The bare forearms, suntanned even in December. It made me wonder if he really did spend all his time in Washington, DC.

"How are you liking Columbia? College life?" he asked over his shoulder, and I quickly turned my eyes away so he wouldn't catch me staring.

"It's good," I answered automatically. And then more honestly, "I don't know how much of a typical college life I'm living, so it's hard to say."

"You aren't a typical person, Isolde," Mark said as we reached the landing. "But it's hard not to look at other people living their normal, messy lives and wonder what it would be like. To be one of them."

It was so like my thoughts that day in the library that I wasn't sure how to answer. It either meant Mark was incredibly perceptive, or that he and I shared this normality-nostalgia in common. I wasn't sure what unsettled me more.

Nearly as unsettling as this almost-small-talk between us. Like I was someone worth getting to know, and not a bride paid for in advance.

The loft was open to the same windows as the lower level

and floored in the same dark wood as below. It was lit by slim wall sconces and furnished with solid pieces upholstered in leather. It took seeing the St. Andrew's Cross for me to realize that the furniture was upholstered in leather for a reason.

Mark was walking over to a lamp in the corner, flicking it on. What I had thought was a wall was actually a cleverly built cabinet, constructed so that it stretched the full height of the space, the seams of the doors concealed. That would be where the implements were kept. The toys.

The things Mark liked to use when he played.

"Have you picked a major yet?" he asked as he opened one of the cabinet doors. I knew from years of sparring and spying at parties that even though his eyes were straight ahead, his attention was completely on me.

As always, that attention was a restless flame licking at my skin. All this time being a cardinal's little mouse, scurrying between millionaires and billionaires and politicians, and I still didn't know why some people had that power and others didn't. Most people were just people, but there was the rare person who somehow felt like *more*, like they saw more, *were* more, and to have them look at you, talk to you, listen to you...

He was a spy. A devil, I reminded myself. It had been his job to coax and cajole and coerce. But it was my job to cajole the devil now.

I had to be careful; I had to play this game better than him.

"Art history with a double major in business finance," I said, running my fingers along the edge of a flat leather platform. It could have been a table, except I saw the cuffs dangling from the corners. A hole in the middle, not big enough for anyone to fall through, but too big to be a mistake.

"It's for a cock," Mark said, having observed me looking.

"Yours?" I asked without thinking, and he seemed very

close to smiling then. There was a pull to his mouth, a certain light to his eyes.

It made me want—well, I wasn't sure.

"I'm not usually the one on the table," Mark said finally, and then turned back to the cabinet, rolling out a drawer. "You should remove your shoes now."

"Not usually?" I asked, bending over to do as he asked, pulling my shoes off and setting them to the side.

"Never," he amended, and he did sound amused now. "Was art history always the plan?"

"The plan was theology," I said, which was true. It had been the middle ground between a business finance degree and joining a convent right after high school. "But my father still insisted on business finance, and so I decided to change to something that would pair better with it after I graduate. The ability to accurately value art or antiques for the private market seemed fairly employable, if niche, and I want to work in a field I'm passionate about before I'm requisitioned for the bank after my father retires."

"Art history seems like a far cry from theology, but I suppose that makes sense." Mark pushed the drawer closed and then closed the cabinet door. I expected to see anything in his hands just then—the things I had learned about— whips, crops, and clamps, things that could be inserted inside me—but when he walked toward me, all I saw was a length of white silk.

"I, um." My brain was firing uselessly, trying to make sense of what he would want with a piece of silk while trying to rebut his mild assertion. "I'm mainly interested in religious art, in liturgical objects and antiques, and their valuation. I'm hoping to work for the Church eventually…"

Mark stopped just in front of me, the silk dangling casually from his fist, and I couldn't pretend it wasn't the only thing I was thinking about.

"Are we starting?" I asked hesitantly.

"We already have," Mark replied.

I stared at him.

"And remember," he said, "this is all for the sake of you learning to act the part. You are not submitting to me truly."

"Right," I said.

We'd already started. He was going to blindfold me.

The floor felt very, very far away all of a sudden.

And then I wanted to slap myself. I'd sparred with men twice my size, I'd battered bags until my knuckles bled, I'd waded through ballrooms of people who had the power to end lives. Why was this such a big deal?

"I'm going to blindfold you," he said. "And then your job will be to trust me. To obey me. Again, only for the sake of this lesson, and if you silently hate me in your heart the entire time, it makes no difference to our purposes, so long as you can school yourself to keep it hidden. That said, I would like to touch you tonight, if that's permissible."

He wanted to touch me.

My face burned. All of me burned. "I—not my—"

I couldn't finish.

"Cunt?" he suggested. "Ass? Tits?"

I nodded.

"Noted. Is everywhere else okay?"

I needed to think about this, but my thoughts were fragile threads that snapped the moment I grabbed hold of them. "Where else would you even want to touch?" I finally asked, and his hand twitched around the blindfold.

"Where indeed," he said enigmatically. And then, "We'll need a word for when you'd like to me stop."

A safe word. Yes, I'd read about those, had assumed I'd need one, even if it would just be used for show.

"Hyssop," I said, the one thing I was sure about tonight.

"Hyssop," he said, and those dark gold eyelashes dropped down and back up. He was surprised, I thought. Something about it had surprised him. "My sacrifice, O God, is a

61

contrite spirit," he quoted, citing the same Psalm I'd been thinking of when I had chosen *hyssop* for my safe word. "A contrite, humbled heart, O God, you will not scorn."

Cleanse me with hyssop and I will be clean.

"Say it when you need to stop. A submissive of mine would have their limits pushed; I would do it on purpose. Concurrently, I would also expect any submissive of mine to be extremely vocal about their limits and boundaries."

"You would push limits on purpose?" I asked doubtfully. That seemed to defeat the entire purpose of limits, according to all I'd read.

"A hard limit, most likely not. But a soft limit? Yes. Entirely."

"Why?"

He lifted a shoulder. "Because I want to. Isolde, if you have been trying to comfort yourself with the belief that I must secretly be a good man—that my transparency so far has proven that I must somehow care about fairness and kindness—then I must ask you to stop. Tonight, if you can." Without waiting for me to respond, he lifted the hand with the blindfold. "May I?"

I licked my lips. After that speech of his, nodding took more effort than anything else I'd ever done. But I managed it. "Yes."

Mark's eyes were the same color as the night sky as he lifted the blindfold to my eyes.

"Since this is only us pretending," he said, wrapping the silk around my head and tying it, "I'm only going to train you as to what I like, and what I would demand from someone who was mine. This won't be a comprehensive education in kink, so if you sense gaps in your schooling, that will be why."

He'd tied the blindfold perfectly, without catching my hair and also without any looseness or remaining visibility. It gave me no physical discomfort, but the disorientation and panic that followed were arresting. I couldn't see—anything.

Not him, not the loft, not any hint of light.

He could kill me, and I wouldn't be able to stop him. He could slap me, kick me, push me down the stairs—

I jumped back as warm fingers found my wrist, but they held me fast, catching my movement before it had even gotten started. His grip wasn't painful, but it was definite, pressing into my skin, and I realized he was measuring my pulse.

"Breathe, Isolde," he said. His voice was firm. Calm. "Breathe."

I didn't think I could. I'd never been this exposed, this helpless, not since I was twelve and walking around not knowing my mother could die at any second. I'd been ambushed by grief, by the jagged shock of disillusionment, and ever since, I'd made myself as aware, as safe as possible.

"Isolde," Mark said, "I'm taking both your hands now. I'm lifting them. Feel what I make you feel."

He lifted my hands and soon my fingers encountered the silk of the blindfold. Loops of it—not knots.

He'd tied the blindfold in a bow. I could pull it off with a mere tug.

He must have felt my hands relax a little at the discovery and he lowered them.

"Your hands are free. The blindfold is not tight. Your safe word is right here between us the moment you need it. Breathe."

He was right. He was right.

I was okay.

Slowly, I found my breath again, one inhale after the other, until my body caught up with my mind. We didn't need to panic.

"I'd like you to get to your knees."

I didn't move at first, abruptly aware of the windows all around us, of how I must be on display in the glass-walled loft. The whole penthouse had felt so private a moment ago, but now being asked to do this, it had transformed in my mind to a stage, a shadow box.

"No one will be able to see up here without a drone." Mark's voice sounded a little farther away now, as if he'd taken two steps back. "And there's no sightline into this space from any of the other buildings nearby."

Once again, he'd accurately read my mind. It set me on edge.

"That was why I bought it," he added.

"So that you could use this place for kink?"

"Among other reasons," he replied. "Kneel, Isolde."

I decided to trust him about the privacy. If anyone would be concerned with sightlines, it would undoubtedly be a former spy. And anyway, I knew I'd have to kneel for him at some point. That was very central in my research; it was a surrender of power, a show of obedience and trust.

In my case, *only* a show.

I dropped lightly to my knees, years of martial arts making the movement easy.

"Good," I heard Mark say. "Now I want you to crawl toward my voice. I'm sitting on the bench near the middle of the room; I'm sure you saw it as you walked up."

I had seen it. But…

"Crawl?" It was a good thing we weren't doing this for real, because I would have made a terrible submissive.

"Yes, crawl," Mark said. There was amusement in his voice again. "This is something you may have to do when we are at the club, so I promise this isn't gratuitous humiliation."

"Why?"

"*Why?*"

"I mean why do you like making someone crawl?"

"Why wouldn't I?" Mark didn't sound angry. If anything, he sounded baffled.

"It's just—" All the kinky stuff had seemed so clear in the

reading he'd sent over. But now that we were *here*… "How is it sexy?"

He answered immediately. "In your case, I think your tits will hang nicely and the ends of all those pretty, blond tresses will drag on the floor. That proud little chin that you tip up at me whenever you think you're being stoic will be facing the floor. Those strong, slender fingers will be splayed as you crawl, and your ass will be up for me to enjoy."

I couldn't find the words to respond.

"And I want you to do it, so that you can tell me what *you* think the appeal is," he added. "It will be your job to act the part, after all, and actors have to find their motivation, or so I hear."

Motivation. Right.

Play the part. Both for Mark and for myself.

I pressed my palms to the floor, feeling how much more vulnerable I was like this. Now I couldn't see *or* make use of my hands.

I shifted my weight forward, and my hair slid off my shoulders. I couldn't see it, but I could feel that Mark had been right—my hair was dragging on the floor as I crawled. And I didn't doubt that my breasts were hanging a little too, the fabric of the sports bra not enough to withstand gravity at this angle.

I moved toward where I'd last heard his voice, where I believed the bench to be, and tried to ignore how awkward it felt. Everything was awkward the first time. A new kata, a new prayer, going through the cafeteria at college. It was practice that bred ease, not rightness. And if I were going to pretend like this was right for me, what would I be feeling right now? Noticing with senses honed from years of eaves-dropping?

Mark's breathing. Yes. It seemed a little rougher now, a little more tightly controlled.

From watching me crawl?

Warmth bloomed on my chest as I continued moving, becoming fully aware of how my backside was moving from side to side as I crawled, how my back had curved. How fragile and humble I must have seemed with my blindfold on and my head down.

If this were right for me, I'd be thinking about my effect on Mark, about how pleased he'd be with my obedience, how aroused he'd be by the sight of me like this, debased and willing. I'd be thinking that if I continued to please him, he might touch me. He might have me spread my knees apart so he could slide his fingers past the waistband of my bike shorts and feel if I were wet. He might bend me over and make use of me until I was limp and boneless and he was satisfied for the night.

And if this were right for me, that thought would have me tormented with need. I'd want it so much that my breathing would speed up and the ache between my thighs would blossom into something full and distracting. There would be nothing I wouldn't do to have Mark keep noticing me.

"Very good," murmured Mark as my fingertips touched his shoes. "You may settle back on your knees now."

I did—and then swayed.

I'd become dizzy somehow. *Me*—the athlete, the martial artist. I'd never been dizzy a day in my life, and yet here I was, my lips and fingers tingling, unable to tell up from down—

Mark caught me before I fell, and with a strength that made me envious and exhilarated at the same time, pulled me onto his lap. I was tucked against the solid expanse of his chest, his arms holding me fast, a palm rubbing my back in firm, vertical strokes.

My face was still tingling, and I was so helpless, and I realized he was asking me a question, something about school, something in a low, conversational tone that was still rough and cool, but warmer than I'd ever heard it.

He'd asked again about my majors, I thought.

"Art history was actually my uncle's idea," I mumbled. I was too disoriented not to let my cheek rest on his shoulder. My legs were draped over his thigh and my heels pressed into the taut leather of the bench. My bottom was planted right in his lap. Something about that felt right. Good. Like Mark was a chair made especially for me.

"It was your uncle's idea," Mark repeated, still stroking my back and cuddling me. His voice was so nice. Feeling him hold me was nice. I was floating.

"He wants me to work for him after I graduate." And then I stopped. Even floating, I knew I shouldn't have said that. I was supposed to have switched to art history because it fit a deep interest of mine, not because a career in assessing religious art and antiquities would be an excellent cover for the real work Mortimer wanted me to do.

But thankfully, Mark didn't seem to notice anything unusual about what I'd said. It wasn't so odd anyway, right? Lots of young people went to work for family members after college. It was only my uncle's position that made it atypical.

"Why did you decide to stay at home instead of living on campus?" Mark asked. "Or getting your own place?"

It was small talk, meant to soothe. He was helping me come back into my own body.

It was working.

"There didn't seem to be much point," I said. My fingers and toes still tingled, but my lips and cheeks no longer did. "The penthouse is much quieter, and I only spend as much time on campus as I have to."

"The point would be having a semblance of a college experience," Mark said. He was still rubbing my back. It was warm. Nice. I wasn't sure anyone had held me this close for this long in years. My mother had been the last, maybe.

"Like you mentioned earlier, I'm hardly a typical college girl. And anyway, what does that even mean, *a college experience*? Drinking with strangers? Having sex with them? Would you really prefer that?"

Mark's hands briefly tightened against me and then relaxed. It happened so quickly that I almost thought I'd imagined it. But I knew I hadn't.

I am possessive by nature.

"I can't say that I would," he said calmly. "Although I do not expect your fidelity until we are married."

I should have felt relief then—not that I had any plans on utilizing that freedom—but there was something deliberate about his choice of words. "You don't expect it…but maybe you would still like it?"

His chest moved underneath me. He'd lifted his shoulder in a shrug I couldn't see. "There's no end to what I would like, Isolde. I learned a long time ago to put some reasonable limits on what I ask of people, because otherwise I will ask the world of them."

His heart beat steadily under my ear. I wondered what *the world* was. If it was something more than fidelity. Something impossible to give.

"Did you have a typical college experience?" I asked after a minute.

He didn't answer at first, the soothing strokes on my back now turning to slow caresses of my hair. "I suppose my freshman year could have been called typical. But then Carpathia happened and we went to war. I enlisted as soon as I could, joined the Rangers eighteen months after that. And I never looked back."

"Never?"

A short exhale. "Even if I'd regretted my choices, there are some doorways you can't walk back through. I could have gone back to school after the war ended with Maxen Colchester's heroics, but the chance of having a typical college experience? That died with the first person I killed."

There was a lull, and then he said, softly, "Do you know

of any doorways like that, Isolde? The ones that can't be walked back through?"

I was all the way back inside my body now, and it was just as well, because my stomach had started to churn. I was about to walk though many of those doorways. Maybe I already had.

I opened my mouth to say so, and then awareness dawned like a cold, white light inside my mind. I was about to give him answers that I didn't want to give, insights into my psyche that I couldn't *afford* to give, not this early in the game. And with the blindfold tied neatly around my eyes, it was easy to see the truth.

I was being interrogated.

By a former spy, by someone who was sitting on such a treasure trove of private information that both the Catholic Church and Wall Street wanted in.

This was an interrogation, and it was working, and it was all because I'd had some kind of vertigo attack while crawling. I couldn't have been more disgusted with myself.

I pushed off his lap, suddenly needing to be apart from him, needing to be on my feet, needing to see. I tore off the blindfold and then flinched as light assaulted me. Even the dim glow up here was too much.

"There's not much you can do to make your sight return faster," volunteered Mark.

I wouldn't glare, I wouldn't sneer, I'd already exposed too much of myself by scrambling away from him like that. By *breaking the scene*, as my research would say. Without a safe word.

Breaking the incredibly intense, deeply painful scene of... me sitting comfortably on his lap.

Shame crawled up my throat. *Weak.* I was weak.

I hated being weak.

"I should have said my safe word," I said woodenly. Mark was already standing, tugging at his rolled sleeves so that his shirt's seams laid in geometric lines on his body again.

"It was your first scene," he said. "I think you did well, given the circumstances. This is all we'll do our first time at the club together anyway. We don't want to give them too much at first anyway."

My eyes were finally adjusting, and I could meet his eyes as I asked, "Who is *them*?"

He slid his hands into his trouser pockets, his stance confident and wide. "Guests of my club. Employees of my club. Everyone involved with Lyonesse, really. They will be curious: I've made use of the occasional submissive, but I've never claimed one. Collared one."

"Collared," I echoed. Yes, I'd read about that too. But somehow I hadn't—it hadn't connected for me—

Mark was watching me carefully. "It's only for show, Isolde. You won't be collared in truth."

Right. Right. But still there was something in me that resisted, that couldn't accept what this was, what Mark's world was built around. "I just...I don't know if I understand this," I heard myself say. I'd nearly passed out from *crawling*, so what was going to happen when we pretended to do anything more?

"You don't understand...what? Collaring? Kink?" His gaze was steady, cold. Indelibly Mark Trevena.

"All of it," I said. The blindfold was still in my hands and I held it up. "Why does anyone choose this? Why does anyone choose *more*, the parts with the cropping and flogging and pain?"

He regarded me with that perceptive stare. "So you've never run until your legs gave out? Never kicked a post or bag until you were crying in pain?"

I went still.

"You've never told a sparring partner that they could go harder with you, that they didn't have to hold back as much?

You've never felt cleansed by pain? Reset by hurt? You've never felt like blood and bruises spelled out a secret story, a hidden story, meant only for you?"

He was guessing all of this. He had to be. He couldn't know that he was right. He couldn't know that above all else, I wanted to be allowed to hurt myself for God.

But this wasn't the same thing at all. I knew it wasn't. It couldn't be.

I didn't answer him; instead, I sat down and began pulling on my shoes, dropping the blindfold next to me. "I'm free for three weeks around winter break, excepting Christmas," I said, without looking at him. "Otherwise, I won't be able to make it to DC until spring break."

"Isolde," Mark said, and I ignored him, standing up and grabbing the blindfold as I did.

"You can text or call. I'll need at least a day's notice to arrange travel."

"Isolde," Mark said again.

I finally looked at him.

I was furious with him. I was furious with myself. I was furious with Mortimer and my father and with my mother for dying and leaving me alone with these men.

"I meant what I said." Mark dipped his head toward the blindfold in my hand. "You did well tonight."

I could have laughed if I wasn't so angry at everything and everyone right now. "I couldn't even sit in your lap for ten minutes. No one is going to believe I have the power to interest you."

I could see him touch the tip of his tongue to his teeth, and then he pressed his lips together. "That won't be a problem," he finally said. "And let me call you a car."

"That would be nice. Thank you." I extended the blindfold to him, and he strode forward to take it. When his fingers brushed mine, I remembered how warm and hard his body had been around me. How his fingers had felt in my hair as he'd caressed me.

I was ashamed I'd let him hold me like that.

I was even more ashamed that I'd liked it.

THAT NIGHT, AS I DREAMED ALONE IN MY BED, SHAME followed me from vision to vision, filling my belly even as I woke up on my stomach, rutting against my mattress as I half-unconsciously rode my way through a panting climax.

seven

On a frigid New Year's Eve, I stepped out of a black car and shut the door. I pulled my coat tighter around me as I looked across the narrow glass and steel footbridge to the island in the Potomac.

This close to shore, the river was a broken mosaic of ice, and I could see loose chunks of it sliding in the channel farther out. On the other side of the bridge was a glass building four or five stories high, its angles striated by deep pink and purple lights. They glowed over the slushy Potomac and against the flat stretch of DC and Alexandria behind them, like the building was a glass casket for a setting sun suspended inside.

There was no way to get there but by foot, by crossing over the bridge.

The piercing wind found its way under my long wool coat, scraping at my thighs and breasts through the thin silk of the dress Mark had sent for me to wear, and it chased me across the bridge as the car idled behind me. Charitably, I wondered if Mark had given the driver instructions to make sure I made it inside safely.

Less than charitably, I wondered if Mark had told the driver to make sure I made it inside, period.

I was here for my first appearance as Mark's fiancée and submissive, and I was determined to acquit myself from our rehearsal a month ago. I wasn't going to let something as simple as crawling knock me off-kilter; I wasn't going to panic just from sitting in his lap.

The tall glass doors slid open automatically as I approached, and I stepped inside the lofty space, my eyes sliding to the stairs, elevator, and smaller door just behind the front desk. The same pink and purple glow from outside was muted in here, softer, complemented by a subdued gold light from strategically placed sconces and pendants. I was the only one in the lobby, aside from the two employees who'd opened the doors and the employee behind the front desk.

Hesitantly, I walked toward the desk, not sure what to say exactly. Was there some kind of sex club etiquette? Would I need to sort out a temporary membership? Could I treat it like a normal meeting? *Yes, hello, I'm here to see the owner? I'm his fiancée, I promise he knows me?*

But the woman—also dressed in black, in a pencil skirt and a leather corset over a silk blouse with a tie-neck—smiled at me as I came forward.

"Miss Laurence," she said warmly. "We've been expecting you."

Of course, Mark would have made all the arrangements. There was a strange feeling that came with the realization, almost like a thrill, to know that he'd thought about me while we weren't together. I had the same feeling whenever he emailed me about my ongoing education in kink, especially when those emails came late at night. I imagined him in bed in that Billionaire's Row penthouse, his phone in his hand and his thoughts on me.

I imagined him here, watching other people play, his thoughts straying to his bartered future wife.

It was a dangerous thing, that thrill. I had to ignore it.

"If you'll follow me," the woman said. She had pale gold skin and thick black hair that was twisted into a neat chignon at her neck. "And over here is our coat check, if you'd like to leave your coat."

The narrow door behind the desk opened and another employee came out, hands outstretched to help me remove my coat. I only hesitated a moment—it would have to come off at some point, anyway. No sense in being bashful about revealing my skimpy outfit now.

But as the young man slipped my coat off my body and the cool air of the lobby brushed against my shoulders and thighs, self-consciousness pulled at me like a cloak made of iron. Mark had chosen my wardrobe tonight, so I knew it would be pleasing to him, but there was no denying the sexual promise it embodied: a short dress made of white silk, with thin straps and a row of fabric-covered buttons marching down the front.

I can easily be undone, it said to anyone looking at it. *I can be lifted up, tugged down, torn off.*

And yet the white...it was practically bridal, especially with the embroidered white ballet flats he'd sent along with the dress, and his very clear instructions to wear my engagement ring. *Bridal* was Mark's point, I supposed.

But neither of Mark's employees gave my barely-covered body a second glance, and I anticipated that a white negligee was the least scandalous of what anyone inside this glass box wore anyway.

I was in Mark's world now, his kingdom, and apparently, I would be its queen. I needed to look like it.

We mounted the floating metal stairs and wound our way up to the second story, where we then pushed through another glass door and into a hallway. Though the lobby had been completely silent, music played in here, a slow, electronic pulse. We passed more glass doors, some frosted, some opaque, and then windows. The windows opened into some of the rooms, and some were full of people laughing and drinking, and some were full of people doing so much more…

A man had a woman bent over a bench and was swinging a paddle at her backside. She was sobbing; he was smiling. And she had her hand between her legs, masturbating herself with a desperation that sent heat flooding through me to witness.

I wrenched my eyes away, face burning. Luckily, my guide was ahead of me and didn't seem to notice. And perhaps it was years and years of situational awareness, of martial arts, of being a social spy, but I couldn't stop looking at the windows. At the people inside, naked or clothed, writhing or stalking around benches, all sorts of pairings and sharings.

The sexual parts of Catholic dogma had never much preoccupied me; I had planned on being a nun, so it wasn't like any of the rights and wrongs would be applicable to me, anyway. But some of the things I saw through the windows tonight quickened my breathing. Made lust kick deep, deep in my belly.

A woman riding another woman's face while she drank something amber-colored from a glass. Two men taking turns with another man, whose cock was trapped in a cage and was leaking semen in long, pearly threads onto the floor between his spread feet. A tangle of people fucking at one man's command while he watched with an unsettling but very sexy sneer.

I had known—of course I had known—that there were things I dreamed about that didn't match up with what my Church said about sex and desire. I knew there were images, impulses, thoughts that came when I saw other girls some-times. Things that, if I'd confessed them, my confessor would have told me were wrong.

So I'd never confessed them—because they didn't matter —because I was going to be a nun.

But what now?

What now when I wouldn't be a nun...or at least not a nun until I'd served long enough for Mortimer to think I'd earned an annulment? What now when my future husband owned a place where the windows were full of this? And not just the women together, but the raw sex, the freedom of it, everyone being with everyone, the paddles and crops and hot wax and people arching in agony with stiff nipples and spread legs, like the agony was everything, everything.

I was flushed and shaken when we pushed out of the hallway to the far door, another glass one. Beyond it, lights danced and bounced, and when the employee opened the door, sound poured in, thick and pulsing and thrumming. Music for dancing instead of fucking.

"Right this way," she called and led me onto a balcony that wrapped around the perimeter of the space. Below us, the dance floor beat like a heart, bodies lifting, dipping, moving as one. Above us were two more floors, also ringed with balconies. I thought I could make out more windows too —more private rooms, these overlooking the raucous party below.

Out here, there were no longer any rooms, but rather nooks open to the space, most of them filled with plush, semi-circular booths, but some filled with rows of chairs, like at the opera. One nook was larger than the others, and there I saw him.

Mark in a black leather armchair that looked like a throne, surrounded by four or five people I didn't recognize.

I followed my guide there, my hands shaking and my stomach twisting, the same way it did right before a judge lifted his hand between me and an opponent at a sparring match. Like for a single, crushing instant, I'd forgotten everything I'd ever known about anything, and I was a complete beginner all over again.

Then Mark looked over and met my eyes, and everything else stopped.

The shaking, the nerves, the vigilant prickle at the back of my neck, constantly reminding me that I was in a new place, a dangerous place, that I had a job to do.

He commanded my attention, and somewhere in the back of my mind, I knew that wasn't good. Around him, I would need to be warier and more watchful than ever—but it couldn't be helped right now as I was seeing him in his domain for the first time. As I was being led to his dark throne like a sacrifice.

Mark Trevena looked like he owned every space he moved through anyway: stalking me in a grimy dojo with bare feet and a rubber knife in his hand; dancing at a rooftop party; wearing rolled-up shirt sleeves in his penthouse. He radiated complete control and dominion wherever he was.

But here? Here in the world he built for himself?

This was beyond an owner in his club, a king in his kingdom. This was more like some shadow god in his underworld, sprawled on his throne while his glittering eyes assessed the tribute being brought his way. The space matched him, reflected him, spoke for him. It was an extension of his will, and I could feel it as I walked toward his nook, the music pulsing, the glass and lights turning everything into a dizzy dream. He was the center of it all, high above his guests, watching them all cavort in his care.

He was the locus, the pivot on which the entire night turned. It was in the way the people in the other nooks watched him, the way people looked up from the dance floor, as if everyone were performing for him. Hoping to impress him.

We stopped in front of his chair, and I allowed myself a quick catalog of the nook before I respectfully dropped my eyes. Mark himself wore a black suit with a black shirt, vest, and tie. With his golden hair and the bored way he lounged back in his chair, he looked every bit the fallen angel.

Next to him was a woman with deep brown skin and close-cropped hair, wearing a dress of something shiny and red. She reminded me of Mark in the way she sat, leaning back with her elbow over the back of her armless chair and her eyebrow arched in a delicate crescent. There was a pale, dark-haired woman next to her wearing a tailored blue suit and a watchful expression that made me uneasy.

Two men sat on the other side of Mark, one in another armless chair in a black tuxedo, the other wearing leather pants and nothing else, kneeling on the floor next to him. Both men had dark olive skin, and the sitting man had a stubbled jaw and shoulder-length hair.

The fifth man was sitting too far back in the shadows for me to see much, other than the suggestion of wide shoulders and gleaming eyes.

"Ah, my bride," Mark said. "Thank you for bringing her to me, Ms. Lim."

"Of course, Mr. Trevena," she said crisply. "Will there be anything else?"

"I think our needs are met for now, thank you." I could feel his eyes on me even though I couldn't see them.

Ms. Lim left us, and I saw Mark's fingers lift from the arm of his chair. I knew what he wanted; we'd exchanged emails about tonight and about my performance. I would kneel; I would be silent unless asked a question. I would call him *Sir* or *Mr. Trevena*. He might touch me, and I'd already sent over a list of my soft and hard limits, so however he touched me would be something I'd already assented to.

I hadn't had as many hard limits as I'd thought. I wasn't sure what to make of that.

Hyssop, I reminded myself as I knelt in front of his black dress shoes. *Hyssop.* I could stop this at any moment, although

I already knew I wouldn't. It was too important for selling our story, the image of me as a financial princess turned submissive turned wife. And if it bothered me that *Isolde Laurence*—black belt, perfect student, devout Catholic—would be reduced to that timeline, I wouldn't let it change anything about my decisions.

Whatever impression of me the world had, I would use it against them to get what I wanted. If they saw me as weak, depraved, unimportant, under someone else's control…all the better for what I needed to do.

"Lovely," the woman next to Mark said admiringly. "If young."

"I didn't know you liked them so fresh and untrained, Mark," said the suited woman next to the first. "You've always gone for more seasoned types. The ones who can keep up with your…tastes."

Mark reached forward and tucked a strand of blond hair behind my ear. I kept my eyes down—Mark himself preferred eye contact with his submissives, he'd said, but around other Dominants, it would be polite to keep my eyes on the floor—until he took my chin and lifted my face to his. In the flashing lights and dancing shadows, it was impossible to tell if his eyes were blue or black. "Andrea thinks you can't keep up with me, darling. Do you think that's true?"

What could be true between us when this was all a lie? "No, sir."

"I think you're right. And half the fun will be showing you my tastes, one by one. Training you to serve me how I like," Mark said. He was still studying my face, raising my jaw even more to study my throat and clavicles. Like he was wondering what a collar would look like there. "Isn't that right, Ash?"

A noise of assent from the shadows.

"Ash here had a submissive of his own when he was young, although I don't think he knew enough to call it that," Mark explained.

"It didn't need to have a name," the man called Ash said. His voice was deep and strong. "We just called it *us.*"

"Hmm," Mark said, running his thumb along my jaw, like a new buyer mapping some freshly bought vase at auction. "And what do you call it now? Or your infatuation with that former vice president's granddaughter?"

A laugh from the shadows. "Hopeless."

The music behind us changed as Mark released my face. I tilted my face back down the moment he did, and he ran his thumb over his fingertips. Our agreed-on signal for *good.*

A thumb in the middle of his palm meant *watch me.* A thumb and a forefinger pressed together meant *stop.* A subtle way for him to guide me through any club etiquette we hadn't anticipated.

The conversation ebbed into club gossip as I stayed between Mark's planted feet, watching the arrow-straight cuffs of his suit trousers shivering on the tops of his shoes. The floor was polished concrete, but I was unbothered by the pain of kneeling there. Kneeling had been the closest I'd come to corporal penance on my own, kneeling on a hard surface for as long as I could stand it, and I had lots of prac- tice embracing the discomfort.

It was cool there in my slip of a dress, so much of my thighs exposed, along with my arms and the tops of my breasts, and after a while, I felt goose bumps pebbling my skin. I wondered how the other submissive on the floor was faring, the shirtless man, but when I tried to slide my gaze sideways without moving my head, I could only see his leather-clad thigh. He didn't seem like he was shivering or anything. Maybe this was another thing subs were expected to endure without complaint.

And then without warning, I was picked up, just like I had been in Mark's penthouse, and nestled in his lap. He didn't miss a beat in the conversation he was having with the man next to him about the increase in international membership applicants, and no one else seemed to react either. My flat-clad feet dangled on the other side of the thick leather armrest; I was resting against his blissfully warm chest with my eyes on my lap. He had a strong arm wrapped around me, also warm, and his free hand drew idle circles on my knee as he spoke.

Like the last time, it was startlingly pleasant. That hypnotic, rainlike scent. His firm body, his chest moving against me as he breathed. And this time I could hear the rumble of his voice against my ear as he murmured back and forth with the other Dominants.

And here with Mark tonight, I understood why Mortimer was so keen for this engagement. No one paid me the slightest bit of mind while they discussed other members and other potential members. Andrea and the woman next to Mark both worked at Lyonesse, I gathered; the man with the kneeling submissive was a regular. Same with the man in the shadows, who barely spoke throughout it all. I could feel when Mark evaded certain answers or changed the angle of his questions just enough to deflect around something, but I didn't know enough about the people or situations they were discussing to say why.

As it was, I knew it was all information my uncle would be ravenous to hear—these wouldn't be the crumbs brought from the parties of the well-heeled on their best behavior, but hills and mountains brought from the darkest corners of their sins.

The Bulgarian attaché who drank martini after martini at the bar and was far too loose with his words.

The Oscar-winning actor who could only orgasm after watching his wife get railed by someone else.

The princess from Averna who came four times a year to have a mistress lock her in a cage.

The megachurch pastor. The socialite. The billionaires and almost-billionaires and former billionaires.

And this was casual conversation. I couldn't even imagine what kind information Mark actually held close and secure.

As they talked, Mark's hand on my leg kept circling, drifting until he was stroking the inside of my knee. Electricity skittered up my thigh—something like ticklishness, like a thrill, but that left warmth in its wake too. His fingers never went any higher than my lower thigh, but it was like the more they stayed there, the more I began to wonder why. During our emailed exchanges over hard and soft limits, I'd said Mark could touch my vulva for the purposes of public display, of performance, and also my backside and breasts. I'd even agreed to full nudity in public, although I had mentioned that I might need time to work up to it.

I'd told myself that I'd agreed to so much because I needed to do more than sell our story to the denizens of Lyonesse; I'd need to eventually win over Mark's allegiance too. His respect, if not his affection. Only then could I count on accessing everything my uncle wanted from Lyonesse.

But the honest truth was that going through that list, limit by limit, was like the first day with a new weapon at the karate school. It was a promise—so many promises, in fact, beckoning me to test myself against them. Promises that were already things I'd longed for under a different context.

Rewards. *Punishments.*

It would all be different, of course, pain for my future husband rather than for God's love, but it called to me nonetheless.

So anyway, I had anticipated him doing more tonight than stroking my knee. The inside of my knee, over and over, slow, slow caresses that made my nipples pull taut under my dress. My clit surged, swelling in abrupt kicks, and I began to invent half-delirious fantasies with my clit at the center of them.

Stroked over my panties. Played with while his free hand pulled the crotch of my panties aside.

SIERRA SIMONE

Fantasies where he'd told me beforehand to wear nothing underneath my dress and then spent the night petting my wet, exposed sex in plain view.

I closed my eyes. What was happening to me? Six months ago, I couldn't believe my father would allow a man like Mark at a party, and now here I was silently keening to be treated like a whore.

Was it Mark? Did he make me want this somehow?

Or had I always been this way?

My knees had parted even more somehow, the hem of my dress falling down my thighs. Anyone could see my panties now, if they wanted, but I didn't care. I wanted Mark to know he could touch me more. If he wanted. If he thought it would be good for our illusion.

Not because I felt my clit like a beating heart between my legs. Not because I was panting softly against his chest while he continued to stroke my leg and talk to the others like nothing was happening.

It wasn't until the DJ on the dance floor put up the countdown to midnight and Mark shifted underneath me that I realized my bottom had been nestled against a thick erection, long enough to make me swallow.

I had left oral, vaginal, and anal sex blank on the question of my limits, not marking *yes* or *no*, marking nothing at all. Saying *yes* would feel too much like saying goodbye to another Isolde, to an Isolde without a honeysuckle ring on her finger. But saying *no* was foolish; to marry Mark and not use every tool I could to win his trust was worse than a half-sacrifice. It would be a wasted one.

And now here I was in his lap, his hard cock pressed against me.

If I *had* marked yes, he would be able to turn me in his lap, unbutton his pants, and—

The countdown got to ten, and Mark stood with me in his arms, setting me on my feet in front of him. Another man

84

was rushing toward our nook, tall and suited with a flag pin in the lapel—and familiar somehow, although the moving lights of the dance floor below made it hard to get a good look at his face. He reached the quiet guest in the shadows just as the building exploded with cheers and *Happy New Years* and the guest yanked him down to his mouth and kissed him passionately.

I looked back up to Mark, who was staring at me with something I couldn't decipher written on his face. He pressed his thumb to my lower lip until my mouth opened for him, and then with a flash of his eyes, he leaned down and slotted his mouth against mine, leaving his thumb between us.

His lips were warm and firm, his breath minty and cool, and something about that thumb was so demanding, almost callous, and I should hate that, I should hate that—

I licked the tip of it, tasting clean skin and a hint of whiskey, and he drew in a sharp breath. And then, like I'd broken through some wall of control, his other hand dug into my hair to hold me still and he pressed his tongue into my mouth.

Our tongues grazed, flickered, fused, and I was panting against him, my hands coming up to fist in the lapels of his jacket to hold myself upright, because my knees were going soft.

My first kiss.

Mark seemed to want every secret my mouth had ever held and searched them out relentlessly. His tongue was stroking and seeking and wicked. His hand in my hair was implacable, and his thumb was still holding my mouth open for him to use.

He pulled my hair the tiniest bit and it was pain and it was ownership, and for a bare, sharp second, everything in the entire world made sense.

And then he dropped his hands and stepped back, licking

his lips. I was pleased to see the fast heave of his chest, the wary look in his eyes.

He was doubting himself now. I'd surprised him.

Perhaps I could play this game with him after all.

Perhaps I could win.

When he spoke, his voice was barely audible over the cheers and music. "Happy New Year, Isolde."

eight

"Sister Mary Alice, I have—I have a question."

Training had just finished for the day, the other students heading to the back rooms to change into street clothes. The middle-aged nun looked over at me from where she was setting rattan canes on a rack.

"Yes, Miss Laurence?"

I didn't fidget or look away—two habits Mortimer had schooled out of me by the time I was sixteen. Actual nervousness or weakness should never be accidentally revealed, he'd told me over and over again. Any betrayal of emotion should be intentional, an act of misdirection. It was in this way that we made sure all conversations turned to our advantage.

I didn't need the conversation to run to my advantage, but I mostly didn't want Sister Mary Alice to think I was asking what I was about to ask out of cowardice.

"I want to talk to you about sex," I said, and her hand paused on the cane she was putting away. I had surprised her.

"Let's go to the office," she replied after a long moment. I nodded, knowing it was for privacy. Classes were done for the night, but people left in clumps and waves, getting caught up

87

in after-class chats or waiting until their bus was closer, and it was a small space. Chances of being overheard were high.

Except when we got inside the office, with the door shut and us settled on either side of the ancient metal desk, Sister Mary Alice pulled out a dusty bottle, followed by two less dusty glasses. I suspected this might have been the real reason we came to the office after all, but I didn't argue when she pushed a glass of something gold across the surface of the desk to me. It made my eyes water when I held it close for a sniff.

It wasn't until she had taken a long, un-nunlike drink that she spoke again. "This is about your engagement."

I nodded. I wouldn't have hidden such a thing from her or Sister Grace, not when it would mean me eventually leaving Manhattan, but the sisters and Uncle Mortimer were thick as thieves anyway, and had been since my mother's death. I'd always figured it was about them keeping an eye on me while Mortimer was out of the country, since no one trusted my father with anything other than my physical wellbeing.

I looked down at the glass, knowing what I wanted to ask and still struggling. I couldn't bear the idea of talking to Mortimer or my confessor about this, and it made more sense to talk to an actual sister anyway, someone already living the life I wanted to lead.

"I never thought that I would be married," I started, my eyes on the liquor rippling in the glass. "But now I will be. I didn't—choose it. For myself. But once I understood why it was important, I agreed to it. So it's not what I wanted, but if I'm going to do it, then I'm going to do right by it. Does that make sense?"

"Your uncle says it will be an enormous gift to the church if you do this," Sister Mary Alice said. "You will be an enormous gift to the church."

We didn't talk often—or ever—about *what* Uncle Mortimer was in the church. A cardinal, yes, and a fixer. But he was something more complicated than that. Ironically enough, I thought if I had to describe his actual work, it would be very close to something like what the CIA did. What Mark used to do.

Information was found. It was acted on.

A necessary job. And I would be a necessary asset.

"I need to decide how real the marriage is going to be," I said, trying to speak levelly, dispassionately. "Uncle Mortimer says he can still furnish an annulment for me, no matter what, so…consummation…is not a barrier to the marriage ending."

"Nor to you taking vows later on," Sister Mary Alice added. "The Holy Father himself has said that a lack of physical virginity is not an issue for anyone seeking the sisterhood."

"Right," I said. I'd known that, but it was reassuring to hear again. I could still be a nun after Mark. I took a drink and then made a face. I didn't drink very often—it messed with hydration, and therefore training, and in social situations, I preferred to be as sharp as possible—but when I did drink, it was more along the lines of a glass of champagne. Not something with the taste of old gasoline.

The middle-aged nun cradled her glass in both hands, the bottom of it resting on the knot of her neatly tied black belt. "I think you need to hear this, so I'll be blunt. Your body is a tool. In every way. You are being called to use it now, like Ruth, like Esther. Like Tamar. This is where God has called you, and so you must sacrifice yourself fully to that calling. Give yourself entirely so that his will be done."

Sacrifice. That word. A word I'd held precious since I first learned it, a word that had become more precious still after my mother had died. There was something beautiful about it, so stunning in its clarity.

Except…

"What if it doesn't feel like a sacrifice?" I asked in a whisper and met the sister's steady gaze. Her slow blink told me she knew what I meant. "What if it doesn't feel like laying something on an altar?"

I thought of New Year's Eve, of being in Mark's lap. Of his thumb against my bottom lip, holding me open for his mouth. "What if I...want to?"

There. I'd admitted it. I wanted to. I wanted sex, and sex with Mark, and not because it would make me better at gathering information or leveraging his club to help the Church, but because he had glittering eyes and large hands and sometimes said things like *I asked for you.*

Sister Mary Alice drank down the last of the bourbon and set the glass on the desk. "I can't tell you much about sex. I've never done it, and I've never wanted to. But *fighting...*" She breathed out, her eyes closing for a second. "I love it. Always have."

She opened her eyes again. "Tell me, Isolde. Does loving fighting make me better or worse at it?"

I'd seen her fight only a handful of times, but she was deceptively strong and quick, with an instinct for seeking out weaknesses. "Better?" I offered.

"Do you imagine that it will be different in your marriage? That offering sex as a necessity, as a neutral transaction, will have the same impact as you wholeheartedly desiring it? I've heard plenty about Mark Trevena; I saw him sparring you that day. He's not going to be fooled by someone closing their eyes and thinking of England—nor, I daresay, would he be interested in it. I think if this arrangement is to have any benefit whatsoever, then it will be precisely *because* you want it. Or parts of it, at least. Does that absolve you?"

"But do you think it absolves me in God's eyes?" I asked quietly, my eyes back down on the bourbon. "It doesn't make me fickle? Or inconstant to him?"

Then Sister Mary Alice did something that she never did. She softened.

"My child. If God didn't want us to be fickle, he would

have never created the ages of seventeen through twenty-seven. Your feelings now don't make you any less who you thought you were a year ago; they only mean that you're getting closer to who you're meant to be a year from now. Five years from now."

She then gave me a sharp smile. "And our God would not send you to battle the dragon without *just* the very sword for the job."

And that night, I emailed Mark an updated list of my limits, with *yes, yes, yes* marked next to all the different kinds of sex.

nine

The here was to be a club anniversary celebration that summer at Lyonesse, and the expectation was that Mark would scene publicly with his new, mysterious submissive.

"Something short, easy," he said when he told me during our second rehearsal in his penthouse. It was the first time we'd seen each other since New Year's Eve.

His eyes were on the snowy expanse of Central Park just beyond his windows. "They don't need more."

"Do you do public scenes often at the club?" I asked. It was a genuine question—I had no way of knowing—but there was a sharp hook in my chest as I awaited the answer.

It was an answer that shouldn't matter, an answer I was pretty sure I could guess, because did I really imagine that someone who built a place like Lyonesse didn't also indulge himself there? Didn't make full use of it?

When his other alternative was a fiancée who knew nothing about what he liked and had barely even been willing to marry him?

He turned to look at me then, framed by Manhattan blanketed in snow, and his eyes were a brilliant blue in the gray winter light. "I do," he said evenly.

"And that's not—" I closed my mouth. I didn't know what I really wanted to ask.

He seemed to know anyway. "It would be stranger if I stopped."

"Oh."

"Do you want me to stop, Isolde?"

And there I was, standing in my sports bra and bike shorts because I was too shy or too stubborn to rehearse without the Lycra reminder that everything between us was false. Because after that knee-quaking kiss on New Year's Eve—even after my conversation with Sister Mary Alice—I wasn't ready to admit how I was starting to feel. There was an instinctive need to wedge some distance between us, any distance at all.

We'd been engaged for over seven months, and I knew next to nothing about him other than that he was fourteen years older than me and had been a soldier before he was CIA. And that he usually drank clear alcohol on ice.

Conversely, he knew far more about me than I knew about him, and in that moment, him looking at me, that kiss last week lingering between us, I couldn't bear for him to know this: that I wanted him to stop doing scenes with other people.

I couldn't even bear for myself to know it.

Wasn't it bad enough that I'd given up my vocation, my purity, my freedom in order to serve God on the darker, thornier path he'd asked of me?

Why did I also have to be drawn—snared? Coveting something so deeply unwise?

Why did I have to *want* Mark on top of everything else?

And what did I want from him, really? To stop fucking other people when we weren't fucking either? When our engagement was a business decision and nothing more?

But now you've told him he can have sex with you, a tiny, petulant voice inside me said. *So why won't he just take you?*

It felt like I'd surrendered something only to have it rejected, neglected. And he absolutely could never, ever know how much that stung.

"No," I said calmly, meeting his gaze again. "I don't want you to stop."

He nodded, something moving in his eyes. He gestured toward the stairs. "Let's get started then."

MARK INTRODUCED ME TO BONDAGE DURING THAT rehearsal. He cuffed my wrists and ankles but didn't secure them to anything else, so I could get accustomed to the sensation of being bound without actually being immobilized. He tied my wrists together with a soft rope, and then later used the same rope to knot a harness over my sports bra.

I sincerely hoped he was writing off my goose bumps and pebbled nipples as something to do with the cool air of the loft, and not what they really were, which was a response to him cinching and constricting me. A response to feeling trapped and held.

It made my belly swim and my heart pound.

Stop, I wanted to demand of my body. *Stop it right now*. The kink was supposed to be yet another sacrifice, a necessary evil, something I did for an illusion. It was not supposed to captivate my thoughts day in and day out. It was not supposed to be the thing I fell asleep thinking about.

I was not supposed be catching my breath from the feeling of cuffs on my wrists.

Luckily, my fiancé didn't remark on any of it, and only

continued to explain how bondage worked, how he'd like our scene this summer to go.

I SPENT THE HOURS LEADING UP TO OUR NEXT REHEARSAL IN the karate school, running forms with the lights off. Two narrow windows let in the late spring sunlight while I flowed through the familiar movements, searching for peace. It was supposed to come; it was supposed to clear my mind and still my thoughts. When it didn't, I did pushups until my arms gave out, and then when my mind still rushed and raced, I went home to my kicking post, covered in tire strips, and began kicking, nearly crumbling with relief as the pain thrummed up my legs and filled me like cold water in a well. Soon I would be still and dark and able to reflect the world back to itself—a perfect mirror, like my uncle had trained me to be.

But as I staggered back from the post, tears burning at my eyelids, Mark's words from before Christmas came to me.

So you've never run until your legs gave out? Never kicked a post or bag until you were crying in pain?

I hated that he could guess that. I hated that anyone could guess anything about me, anyway, because I wanted to be unknowable, a forgettable doll in Manhattan's glass and steel dollhouse, but that he could guess *that* of all things…

He made me feel so powerless with what he could see sometimes. And if he could see that, then could he see that I was choosing this marriage for reasons that had nothing to do with my father? Would he be able to tell when I started handing information off to my uncle, sifting through Lyonesse's vast troves of information for anything that could help the Church?

I got to Mark's penthouse determined to shield myself better. He needed to see only what I allowed him to see—someone hesitant but open, someone slowly turning into a real partner for him.

A tense shiver ran down my spine and the backs of my arms as I reminded myself of that last part. Mortimer hadn't said as much the last time we'd talked over the phone, but our conversation had made me realize that I would get more done with Mark's trust than without it, and if that were true of only trust, then what could I do with affection? Infatuation?

I was hardly Mata Hari; seduction was probably past what I could do with an easy mark, and my future fiancé with his depth of experience and distinct tastes was hardly that. But I could give Mark something very few submissives could, and that was being his tabula rasa, his to mold into whatever he wanted. If I could parlay that into him feeling something for me—even mild attachment—it would prove far more useful than a transactional relationship. And there was also what he'd admitted at dinner that first night…

I asked for you.

I wanted you.

So the game was to make him think I was beginning to crave his kinky world, and him in it, to make him think that he'd accidentally acquired for himself the perfect wife by training me to pretend to be one.

And I wasn't going to be jealous of his other lovers and play partners. And I wasn't going to balk at whatever he asked of me. And I wasn't going to lose sight of why I was here. This was my vocation now, my calling. My sacrifice and narrow way. Like Esther, I would scrawl out God's will onto the world not in the light, not in the shadows, but in the faint glow of a king's bedroom.

I could do it. I could make Mark think I was feeling one thing while I truly felt another.

Except the next night in Mark's cool, dark penthouse, I

couldn't seem to find the certainty I'd felt coming here. I couldn't untangle my body's responses as he cuffed me and connected the cuffs to the leather upholstered platform in the middle of the room. I couldn't separate pretending from *feeling* as he leaned over me, bracing his hands on either side of my head, and I was swallowed by the shadow of those wide shoulders and thick arms.

"We will try light impact tonight," he said. "And some touching. I'll do a mix of flogging and spanking during our scene this summer, and I want you to get used to how they feel, so we can be convincing."

"How convincing will we need to be?" I asked. The research materials Mark had sent over last fall had contained several videos of kinky scenes, and impact play in particular seemed difficult to fake.

"I will pull my strikes as much as I can, but I'll need to leave some welts and marks for it to be believable," admitted Mark. "How do you feel about that?"

"I feel okay with it," I said. It was strange to be talking so matter-of-factly about this while I was spread on a table and cuffed to its corners. While a soft buzz was starting under my skin, tickling my lips and the tips of my fingers and toes. I recognized it from the time I'd nearly fainted from crawling, and tried to push it back. There was no reason being bound to a table should make me feel like the world was falling away. No reason it should make me want to laugh and cry at the same time.

"You'll have your safe word, and it'll be choreographed in advance," Mark said, all cool assurance as he straightened up. He reached for the flogger he'd set next to me on the table and explained its composition and function to me in concise, direct terms.

Cowhide, thirty tails, each twenty-four inches long. Suede was softer; oiled leather would paint me black and blue. I'd be struck with the lower quarter of the falls—sometimes the very tips, which would feel sharp and stinging—and sometimes with more length, for a thuddier impact.

I held onto myself and my earlier determination while I was cuffed to the table. Even as the buzzing under my skin amplified, even as he demonstrated what he was saying with flicks and quick, soft strikes to the tops of my thighs and my breasts. But when he moved me to the St. Andrew's Cross, re-cuffing me so that my feet were spread and my arms were stretched above my head, the world started to spin too fast for me to spin with it.

I was dizzy, already leaned forward against the padded cross for support, and when he flicked the flogger across my back for the first time, my eyes slid closed without me meaning for them to. He was narrating what he was doing, explaining where he'd strike and the places he'd avoid, and it was only the rough coldness of his voice that kept me some-what tethered.

Otherwise, I might have floated right up into the air.

You cannot, I tried to remind myself. *You have to keep a clear head.*

But I wasn't an actress, and even if I were, maybe it wouldn't have mattered. Something about the things Mark did—it was more potent than any liquor Sister Mary Alice kept in her desk, as heady as the most euphoric, agonized prayer. Even through my bike shorts, the flogger bit me and pushed me. Reached into a place in my soul that I normally only let God see.

"After a good deal of this," Mark said after several minutes of flogging my shoulders, backside, and thighs, "a submissive would be lost in their own world. Limp. Docile." He wasn't flogging me anymore, and I could hear him as he came closer. He was close enough now that I could feel his breath on my neck, ruffling the hair that had escaped from my twin French braids.

"You could flog them more," he said, his voice low, "or get

something worse, a crop or a cane. You could get them to beg you for it. You could get them to beg you for anything."

His words were as seductive as the flogger tails had been. Maybe more.

You could get them to beg you for anything.

"What do you do?" I managed to ask.

A low noise, like a hum. "I like the begging. But now is also when a sub is the sweetest to touch."

His hand came to my waist, large and warm, and then slid to the front of my stomach. My skin was exposed between my sports bra and my shorts, and goose bumps trailed behind his fingers.

"Of course," he went on, "since we're only putting on a show, I'll only make it look like what I'd usually do."

"And what's that?" My voice was a whisper now.

His fingertips found my navel. Drew circles around it. "I'd reach between your legs and check to see if your clitoris was erect, and if it was, I'd begin toying with it." His fingers echoed his words, rubbing a spot just above my navel. "I'd then see how wet you were for me. Wet enough to take my fingers, perhaps…"

Those same fingers swirled at the rim of my belly button, making me suck in a breath. I couldn't move, I was cuffed to the cross, and anyway, Mark was behind me, a wall of Italian cotton and tailored wool and low words.

"Or maybe wet enough for a cock. Not that I'd give it to you; you'd have to show me you'd been good enough for it."

His fingers dipped into my navel now, and I made a noise, a barely-there moan. I prayed he didn't hear it.

"I'd make you come until that cunt was nice and flushed for me, and then I'd uncuff you from the cross and carry you to the table. I'd spread your legs so that everyone could see between them and see what you'd done."

I could barely breathe. "And then what?"

His hand dropped from my stomach, and I wanted to cry.

"It's hard to say," he said, his voice sounding farther away, and also a little more detached. "I suppose it depends on the sub. And the scene."

I was too dizzy and dazed to push away the images that came to mind: Mark with his hand between my legs, Mark forcibly pushing my thighs apart for the pleasure of others. Him allowing them to touch me…use me…

"You may feel some pins and needles when your arms are lowered," Mark warned as I felt his hands on the cuff of my right wrist. He sounded oblivious to the effect all this was having on me. "That's normal. I won't keep you in a position like this overlong; once a sub starts getting dosed with neuro-transmitters, I find they start to sag in the cuffs, and that's when I start worrying about circulation."

He was talking as if everything were normal, as if every-thing were the same.

As if I weren't about to topple over sideways from dizzy, delirious sensation after he uncuffed me.

Get it together, Isolde. I wanted him to think I was succumbing to all of this, but that wasn't permission to fall over dead when the man touched my belly button—

"I think we're ready," Mark said, unlocking my final ankle and then standing up. I stayed slumped against the cross. "We didn't rehearse any spanking, but I trust we'll be able to pick it up in the moment. Do you have any questions for me, Isolde?"

I'd always been a good student, a diligent one, but I couldn't bear to be in the lesson any longer. I shook my head —still dizzy— refused his offer of water and toast, and then practically bolted from his penthouse.

When I got home, I locked my bedroom door, laid flat on my back, and with only a second's worth of shamed hesita-tion, spread my legs like someone had made me do it. My entire life, I'd thought masturbation was bad, a sin, but maybe that didn't matter for me anymore. If I was willing to fuck a man, kneel half-naked on the floor for him in front of his friends and employees…surely this was the least of the sins I'd be committing in the name of service and sacrifice.

Not that it mattered. There was no stopping my hand as it swirled a long touch around the rim of my navel and then slid into the tight stretch of my bike shorts. I closed my eyes and tried to think of nothing as I found the small pearl of my clitoris.

But I didn't think of nothing. I thought of large hands prying my thighs apart. And of a cold, cruel voice asking me if I'd been a good enough girl to earn it.

ten

On the first of May, I came home from campus to find my bedroom filled with greenery. Flowers licked delicately between the leaves, yellow and white and pink, and the room was filled with their scent— faint vanilla, soft fruit. That lovely, green *something* that came with fresh leaves.

Breathing it in felt like breathing in something important that I'd forgotten.

There was a handwritten note on my bed.

> ISOLDE,
> I REGRET THAT I CANNOT BE IN MANHATTAN TODAY.
> HAPPY BIRTHDAY, AND I'M LOOKING FORWARD TO OUR
> SCENE AT LYONESSE VERY MUCH.
> YOURS FAITHFULLY,
> MARK
> P.S. I THOUGHT I'D HEDGE OUR BETS WITH THE
> HONEYSUCKLE.

I looked around the room, green and fresh and lovely, and

didn't bother to fight the smile pulling at my mouth. Honey-suckle portended a good marriage, he'd told me at our dinner, and now he'd filled an entire room with it.

He wants us to have a good marriage.

That could mean anything, and I absolutely should not decide what it meant while surrounded with fresh flowers that he'd somehow magicked into my room.

Next to the note, there was a gold box, long and flat, tied with a wide black ribbon. I untied it and opened the box, my lips parting as I beheld the knife nestled in gold velvet inside. A fixed blade, maybe five inches long, and slender. The steel was dark and rippled, and the handle looked like it was made of bone. It was inlaid with gold and rubies, both of which twisted their way up from the guard to the narrow butt of the handle. The same pattern was etched onto both sides of the blade, ornate and lush and unmistakable.

Honeysuckle. Branches, flowers, fruit.

I held it in my hand, switching my grip back and forth, testing its weight. It was light and skinny, and even in a sheath, would fit easily inside a boot or up a sleeve. Every-thing about its shape and dimensions was utilitarian and meant for use…but it was so decorated, so lovely a thing, that the idea of using it was absurd. Like using a Ming vase to collect rainwater under a leak in the ceiling.

But…

But I loved it. It felt perfect in my hand, the size, the weight. Even the bone felt right, slightly warmer than the gold and rubies against my palm.

There was a note inside the box too, inked in a neat, precise hand.

REMEMBER, REVERSE GRIP IS FOR WHEN YOU MEAN IT.

— M

SOME PEOPLE HAD MEN WOO THEM WITH JEWELRY, WITH ROSES and orchids and champagne. I had a man who sent me knives and parasitic flowers.

I was smiling the rest of the day.

eleven

SIX WEEKS LATER

"**E**verything is ready for your visit," Mortimer was saying on the phone. "Do you have everything you need on your end?"

I thought of the suitcase currently sitting in the middle of my DC hotel room. Neatly packed with clothes for a hot Roman summer, along with toiletries and one very beautiful knife. "Yes," I said. "And more."

"Marvelous." My uncle sounded delighted. "We'll talk more when you arrive. I'm so excited to see you, my child."

We said our goodbyes, and I ended the call, pacing a little around the sumptuous waiting room I'd been put in when I'd arrived at Lyonesse thirty minutes ago. Tonight was Lyonesse's anniversary celebration, and then tomorrow I'd fly from DC to Rome. I would finally get to join my uncle and help him with his work for the first time, even if it was only for a few weeks, and I couldn't wait. A taste of the life I could have had without Mark, maybe, serving God in the heart of his earthly kingdom.

The door clicked open, and I turned to see the woman

who'd sat next to Mark on New Year's Eve. She was wearing a black pencil skirt made of something shiny—latex, maybe, or PVC—and a white blouse. She had a narrow jaw, high cheekbones, and eyes that tilted up at the corners. Her mouth —wide and full—was painted a red that brought out the jeweled hue in her deep brown skin. Something about her reminded me of Mark and the man who'd sat behind him, and it took me a minute to realize what it was.

Her expression. Lifted brow, neutral mouth.

It was the way Mark looked at me when I was cuffed to his furniture.

I cleared my throat. "Hello. I'm here for the celebration."

"I know," she said and closed the door behind her. "Mark sent me to help you get ready. He'd do it himself, but he's glad-handing the early guests. I'm Dinah, the club manager."

I took her offered hand as she approached. "I'm Isolde Laurence."

"The fiancée," Dinah said. "I can't say I've wrapped my head around this engagement yet, but anyone brave enough to let Mark collar them is someone I'm honored to meet." She gave me a small smile. "God have mercy on your soul, and all that. Now, follow me to your dressing room. I believe Mark has already set aside everything you'll need."

Walking with Dinah through the club was like walking with the mayor. People stopped her, called out to her, fell in step beside her and handed her things. Though the celebration wouldn't officially start for another hour, there were already plenty of small catastrophes brewing: the bar was out of the vintage cognac the Canadian ambassador preferred; there was some mix-up with a C-drama actor's room and the number of submissives waiting for him there. Some of the early guests were already drinking heavily enough that they'd need to be barred from the playrooms later. A lube-warmer had broken in a playroom and no one could find a replacement.

Dinah handled it all easily, naturally, with the knowledge and authority of someone in her element, and I wondered how she'd come to work for Mark in the first place. Was this the kind of position that could even be advertised for?

"How much has Mark told you about Lyonesse?" Dinah asked, and I wondered how much he'd told her about *us*, about the real nature of our engagement.

With a glance at the easy set of her shoulders and relaxed expression, I decided to answer truthfully, if vaguely. "Not much. Most of our conversations involving kink have been about us, not the club."

"Well, then, since you've only been here once before, let me give you a proper introduction to how the club works." Dinah stopped by an elevator and pressed a button. The doors opened immediately.

"Lyonesse is not a brothel," she said as we stepped inside and she selected our destination. The doors closed silently and we whooshed down two floors. "Legally speaking, guests don't pay us for sex."

"Ah," I said. Doubtfully.

"I know, it looks like that on the face of things. But our guests are members, and as members, they are allowed to use our facilities for their needs. They're also allowed to do anything they'd like with those facilities, including fuck inside them."

"But you have submissives who work for the club." The elevator doors opened, and we stepped out into a glass-walled space overlooking the open center room of the building, the same one Mark's nook had overlooked on New Year's Eve.

"We have Dominants too," said Dinah. "But our members don't pay for our employees' use. They are here to serve in the same way the bartenders and kitchen staff serve —as part of a member's benefits and part of the experience Lyonesse provides. No extra payment required."

We were walking to the far end of the space now, toward

a glass door leading to a hallway. The room below was empty for now, the stage at its front curtained off from the rest.

"Of course, this gets sticky from the law's perspective. Lyonesse dodges this in two ways. Firstly, that our Dominants and submissives work for our club *only* to meet the kink needs of members. Meaning that they are there explicitly for a scene and nothing else. Kink does not have to equal sex, and indeed, we do have several members who have a need for kink separate from sex. If a member would like sex along with a scene, this is a distinct and private negotiation between the Dominant or submissive and our member. Our Dom or sub is not paid for consensual and spontaneous sex, of course. But if they happen to receive gifts of money or valuables after…"

We reached the door and Dinah opened it with a press of her narrow silver watch to a pad next to the door.

"Would that really hold up to scrutiny?" I asked. "Especially if Lyonesse were to facilitate those private negotiations?"

"Of course not," Dinah said crisply as she stopped in front of a door. "That's why Mark bribes and blackmails half the district's officials to look the other way."

"Oh."

"It's only half, because the other half are already members here," Dinah added with a wicked grin.

My belly flipped to see her smile. Did I have a secret weakness for wicked grins? Or just for beautiful Dominants in general?

"You'll see your things are already waiting," said Dinah, opening the door to a dressing room paneled in black wood and with a single window looking over the low DC skyline. "The glass is one-way, don't worry. Just dress, and soon you'll be led to the stage and your scene. You and Mark are the first on tonight, and the crowd will be easy to impress. They worship Mark, so all you have to do is be pretty and helpless and they'll be creaming themselves."

I walked over to the open closet door. There was a short white dress inside, thin enough to be translucent, along with a long white ribbon for my hair. There were no shoes, but there was a pair of boy shorts. My eyes lingered on them, not sure what to think. I appreciated that Mark was giving me these small nods to modesty, that the plan was to pretend as much as possible, but if I wanted him to feel *something* for me, then we needed to…progress.

Physically.

Unfortunately, I was also certain that Mark would not like it if I went off script and disobeyed his tacit command to wear what he wanted.

"Thank you," I told Dinah, already taking the dress from the hanger.

"Happy to help," she said, and then she paused with her hand on the door, her coffee-brown eyes on mine. "You are the most composed submissive I've ever seen—composed enough that I'm already wondering what it would take to fracture all that gorgeous control of yours. Just be you out there on the stage, and I know you'll give us all a hell of a show."

And then she left me to dress alone.

THE PALE WOMAN FROM NEW YEAR'S EVE CAME TO COLLECT me, and then together we went downstairs to the backstage area. I shivered in my short white dress, and she—Andrea was her name—looked over at me with a gaze so disapproving that I could feel it burn along my skin. But she didn't speak, and I didn't either, feeling suddenly very young. Just a college student in a tiny white dress that barely covered my backside, my feet bare and my hair tied in a simple braid and bound with a ribbon. And she was a grown woman, every bit an adult with her tailored suit and perfectly waved hair.

What must she think, I wondered, about Mark being engaged to nineteen-year-old me?

What must they all think?

From backstage, I could hear someone giving a speech to the room, the crowd laughing and applauding at all the right moments. It was dark back here, the only light coming in from the stage lights, and I had the surreal moment of briefly not recognizing my own life.

Isolde Laurence, banking heiress—Isolde Laurence, who wanted to be a nun—was about to walk onto a stage wearing nothing but a flimsy silk nightie and allow herself to be cuffed to a cross and flogged. In front of hundreds and hundreds of people.

The person talking ended their speech and the stage went dark. Andrea took my upper arm and led me onstage, and I resisted the instinct to pull free, to twist against her wrist in a way that would immediately break her hold.

Play helpless, play weak. It's just part of the game.

But it chafed all the same.

I was led to the middle of the stage and left there, standing in the near-darkness, listening to the whistles and calls of the crowd. They were hungry for the night to begin, for the depravity to commence, and when the lights came up to reveal me standing there, looking lost and nervous, they erupted.

I breathed into my stomach, calming my nerves by staring back at them, by finding the exits behind them, by counting the rooms on the upper levels that looked out onto the stage.

They were just people. Just people eager for sex and for violence, and they were no different from the Manhattanites and Londoners my uncle had trained me to spy on. And in some cases, they were literally no different because they were in fact the same people.

Hyssop. Hyssop. It was a chant in my head. *Hyssop.*

I could stop this at any point.

Hy—

Mark stepped out from the other side of the stage, again in an all-black tuxedo.

The crowd lost it.

Screams, shouts, roars—the space was now a well of noise, and all of it in adulation of its leader. Mark nodded at them, and then his blue eyes slid over to me. I swallowed. It had been three months since I'd last seen him, and the effect seeing him had on me was alarming. Embarrassing.

But effective, perhaps, because I saw him notice my fast breathing, my tongue darting out to wet my lower lip, and those blue eyes darkened.

He strode over to me, long, easy steps in that fallen angel tuxedo of his, and moved between me and the crowd.

"Ready?" he asked, looking down at me.

The stage lights were directly behind him, turning him into nothing more than a silhouette. I could only make out the immaculate sweep of his hair away from his face, the outline of his carved cheekbones.

"Yes." I looked down at his dress shoes. The light was hurting my eyes.

"Say your safe word if you need to," he said, and he sounded more serious than I'd ever heard him. "I'll need to make tonight look convincing."

"Give me what you'd give any submissive, Mark." I met his eyes again. "Sir, I mean."

"But you're not any submissive," he said, leaning close to murmur in my ear. "You're going to be my wife."

The way he said *wife* sent a hot, electric thrill racing down my spine. He said it like it was a personal fantasy of his—the filthiest pleasure he could imagine.

A delicious tension stole up my thighs as he stepped back and turned to face the crowd. He said nothing, but he didn't need to. They fell silent on their own, held captive by his attention and his desire.

Music began to fill the room, low and pulsing, and then Mark took my hand and bent his head over it. His lips, warm and soft, brushed over my knuckles, and the crowd stirred, loving it, loving this small, gallant kindness before I was strapped down and punished.

It was hard not to love it too. Hard not to love the way he looked at me through his lashes as he lifted his lips, the way he tugged me closer to him with his eyes burning into mine. His other hand found my hip and then my ass, squeezing it roughly through the dress. He tugged it up, exposing my boy-short-covered backside, and then looked over my shoulder and down at what he'd revealed, giving me a quick, hard slap.

The room roared its approval as I gasped. The pain was sharp and short, there and gone again, but it still sent adrenaline zinging through my blood. If this were a sparring match, I'd shake it off and put my guards back up to fight again. But this wasn't a sparring match, or even a fair fight. I was consecrated to pain tonight. I was an offering to it.

Just like I'd hoped to do for God, I would hurt for my future husband. And hope that I could keep my head clear as my heart sang with joy for it.

Mark wrapped his hand around my braid and walked me over to the St. Andrew's Cross in the middle of the stage. His expression was as cool as ever, but there was something different about him in front of his club, something a little more energetic. His strides were longer, his shoulders looser. When he cuffed me to the cross and then turned to ask the crowd if he should get his flogger, his voice was dripping with a smooth, seductive malice I'd only heard once before: at my father's rooftop party.

He was performing for them. Their king. Their chosen devil.

And they loved it. As he smacked my bottom again before

he stepped away to get his flogger. As he came back and used my braid to tilt my head to the side. As he ghosted his lips over my neck until I squirmed and then bit down hard enough to make me cry out.

Their cheers and calls mixed with the low, tugging bass of the music, and when the flogger's tails licked at my back for the first time, the noise was deafening. There was another rush of adrenaline, and everything felt sharp, so very sharp. The noise, the lingering sting from Mark's bite, the air brushing the underside of my bottom, it all reminded me that I was on display. That the people on the floor could undoubtedly see up my dress, see right through it under these bright lights. They could see me flinch as Mark struck my back again; they could see the flogger's kisses surely rising on my skin right now.

Hyssop.

Hyssop.

Cleanse me with hyssop and I will be clean...

Mark's lazy, exploratory flicks began to change. They came faster now, like needles dancing over my shoulder blades, all cutting heat and sting, and I was shifting on the cross without realizing it, trying to escape the feeling when it came, and then seeking it out when it left. I didn't know what I wanted, if I wanted it to go or if I wanted it to come, and then the flicks changed again, no longer solitary strikes but a rhythm, a razor rain on my back. Unceasing, fast, relentless, and I couldn't catch my breath, couldn't find my center, couldn't find anything except for him behind me and the pain burning like hellfire along my skin.

He stopped and I sucked in the cool air, dizzy from lack of oxygen. The crowd was quieter now, as if enthralled, and Mark paced behind me like a cat, patient and deadly.

It was only a handful of seconds before my thoughts cleared and I could lift my head—which was when he struck again. Fire upon fire, painting my shoulder blades red, giving me wings made of stinging, scarlet welts.

Needles under my skin, my center slipping away, breath long forgotten.

The heat was everywhere: my back, my throat, my chest. Swirling like liquid fire in my belly and simmering between my spread thighs.

Mark paused again, then paced patiently behind me again. There was a method to his pauses, but I couldn't figure it out. I hadn't moaned or grunted. I hadn't collapsed against the cross or whispered for him to stop.

Maybe it was like music, with movements and lulls and crescendos. Or maybe it *was* like sparring, coming together in a flurry of strikes and then breaking apart again.

Whatever the method was, it matched whatever was happening inside me. The world had gone from sharply vivid to blurred to the point of abstraction. The music had sunk into my bones along with the heat from his flogger; I was breathing in time to it, breathing in time to his strikes; they were all the same thing now. Breath, music, pain. My breasts ached as if by proxy, craving the leather too, and my clitoris was aching even more.

Another pause, and then—

Mark lifted up the hem of my dress, a gesture entirely for show, given how short it was. The crowd screamed, and then the flogger snapped against my exposed ass, harder than it had on my back. I jumped in my cuffs, and the crowd screamed louder. Again I felt the leather, again I heard the screams, and it was all so strange, because they were screaming to see me played with for their amusement, for their pleasure, but it was almost like they were screaming *for* me, like their voices were my own, and they were sharing this with me, the highs and the lows, the burn and then the insidious heat that followed after.

Mark spared nothing, it felt like, giving me all his strength, all his cruelty, and I was crying, shivering, but something else was happening too, the same thing that happened when I kicked the kicking post at my school until I couldn't stand anymore, the same thing that happened whenever I knelt on the cold marble floor of my church until I was numb…

The pain was tugging me under or pulling me up, I never knew which, and it was cold and it was hot, and it was sluicing over me and it was burning me alive; it was cleansing me with water and searing away my impurities. My breath was like a flower furling and unfurling in my stomach, the imperceptible stillness between each inhale and exhale beckoning like heaven itself. God was here, around me. Inside me, a fullness in my veins and a joy nestled in the close, wet chambers of my heart.

This—this was what I had begged my uncle for. The gift of feeling God through pain, of feeling my transgressions burned away, my heart cleansed and full. And here I was, ecstatic with it in full view of hundreds, sagging into Mark's chest as he dropped his flogger to the floor and uncuffed me from the cross.

He swept me up into his arms, and I blinked up at him. In the bright stage lights, his eyes were a brilliant blue, almost aqua, a warm and clear sea.

"Are you going to spank me now?" I whispered.

That had been a plan—yes, *the* plan. The plan made a thousand years ago. Flogging, and then spanking. He would pretend to make me come after. I was supposed to fake my pleasure, and the subtler, the better, he'd told me. No Meg Ryan theatrics.

He looked down at me. "Yes," he said so that only I could hear him under the music and the crowd. "Do you remember your safe word?"

"Yes. But I won't use it." My murmurs sounded dreamy even to myself; I sounded drugged. "I want you to hurt me more."

Something moved behind his eyes, gone before I could identify it. And then he bent his head and licked the side of my face.

The crowd roared their approval, and I shivered as I understood what he'd done.

He'd licked the tears off my cheek.

I was carried to a padded leather table and bent over it without ceremony, my dress impatiently shoved up past my hips and a large hand coming between my shoulder blades to pin me to the table. The room behind us was desperate now, a keening, hungry edge to their calls and cheers, and the first hard smack to my ass came with thunderous applause.

Mark didn't pause to acknowledge it, didn't slow down in the least. His hand came again and again, harder than the flogger, and faster too—strike after strike after strike.

On the sixth one, I cracked, letting out a grunt, and on the seventh one, I moaned so loudly that the audience heard. They stilled, going quiet, treating themselves to my choked-off cries and groans, which were fast turning into sobs.

It hurt so badly, and it felt so *fucking* good—like being filled with cold, clean water, filled with stillness and peace, and also like being purified like gold in a fire. The pressure against my aching breasts felt like destiny, and my nearly exposed cunt as I was bent over the table felt like fate.

Mark's hands were on my back and punishing my backside, but his touch was everywhere, his *will* was everywhere, and there was no unspooling that from any other feeling, the cleansed feeling, the God-feeling, the euphoria of it all... Each strike was a fresh surge of heat to my sex, an invisible mouth licking me between the legs.

I lost count after the eleventh strike, my body shivering and my heart sliding into my stomach, and I wondered if the lights were bright enough that the audience could see the shape of my pussy through my underwear. I wondered if they could see that I was flushed and slick there. I wondered if

Mark could see. I wondered if he wanted to fuck my cunt, right now on this stage, pulling my underwear down to my ankles and unbuttoning his tuxedo pants and impaling me in front of everyone here. I wondered what it would feel like, him sliding thick and merciless inside me, taking his pleasure, using my hole until he filled me full.

I wondered if he'd leave me there after, for everyone to see how I'd been used.

I almost didn't realize it was happening as it was building, the rest of my body was so hot and tight—but it was unmistakable, urgent. Necessary.

I was about to have an orgasm.

I was about to have an orgasm in front of hundreds of people, with my dress shoved up around my hips and my bottom red from my future husband's hand.

No. *No*, that couldn't happen—that wasn't me, that wasn't supposed to be how this worked. I was supposed to *pretend*; I wasn't supposed to do this for real, be this for real—

Hyssop.

I could say it. I could stop it before it happened, claw back whatever dignity I possibly could before my body betrayed me. It was as simple as one word. Two syllables.

I could say it, and I believed that Mark would honor it.

But I didn't say it. I didn't say anything.

I grunted and I cried. I gasped against the leather top of the table.

And then pleasure ripped through me like fabric tearing in two, sudden and violent and irreversible, and my pussy clenched tight and then released. Again, again—clench, release—surges that stole my very breath, until I was panting, mouth open against the leather, shuddering and shaking and crying.

I'd never felt anything like this. Not with my furtive grasps toward pain with my kneeling and my kicking post. Not during my tentative flirtations with pleasure, alone in bed with my hand between my legs and my face turned toward the wall. Not even in my dreams, knotted and coiled as they were.

This—this was new.

And it was breaking me, soiling me, tearing all my good and dignified intentions in half.

Mark was still spanking me through it, and after a final strike that sent a ragged moan from my lips, I felt him step closer. He rubbed a hand over my abused backside, sending sparks trailing after his touch.

"What do you think?" he asked his admirers in that cool, seductive voice. "Has she pleased me? Has she earned something in return?"

They went wild, of course, but I wasn't paying attention to them. I was only paying attention to Mark's hand sliding under my ribs to find my throat, to him pulling me up against his chest and turning us so that we faced the crowd. A thick erection dug into my back; he was hard from beating me. My sadistic fiancé.

His free hand found the hem of my dress and moved up my thigh to cup my pussy.

I shivered against him, the pressure and heat of his hand so wonderful that I wanted to push against it, grind shamelessly against it. Make him hold me there forever. Even in front of everyone here. Maybe especially in front of everyone here.

Distantly, I knew I would be appalled by these thoughts later, but I didn't care, I couldn't care. I was pressed against Mark Trevena with his hand between my legs and all I wanted was *more*.

I knew, also distantly, that he would probably be able to guess the effect the scene had on me, and whatever shred of self-preservation I had left was begging me to stop this before he could find out. Begging me to keep it our secret, because once he knew the effect this had on me—that *he* had on me

—he would never unknow it. And surely he would use it for his own agenda somehow.

I would, in his shoes.

But I didn't stop him as his hand moved—with the approving screams of the audience—to the waistband of my boy shorts. I didn't say my safe word. I just shivered against him, his other hand still collaring my throat, as he dipped his fingers past the elastic and down to my pussy.

He was trying not to touch me, I could feel that right away; he was trying to keep a nearly invisible distance between his touch and my skin. But my boy shorts were tight and the angle was strange, and his fingertips brushed once over my vulva.

He froze behind me, his hand going still, and again, his fingertips skated over my slick seam. Intentionally this time.

A rough exhale near my ear.

"Did you come?" he asked in a low voice.

I hesitated, and then gave a tiny nod.

Another exhale.

He didn't speak again.

Neither did he touch me again. He lifted his hand the barest amount and then pretended to masturbate me in front of the audience until I pretended to have an orgasm.

I wished I had the courage to ask him to touch me for real, to make me come for real.

I wished I had the courage to say *take me, use me, press my face into the floor and make me scream.*

I could hate myself for that.

And maybe I already did.

twelve

THE NEXT WINTER

I was staring out the window of my family car, seeing not Manhattan in winter, but that Lyonesse stage, the lights, the crowd.

Mark had carried me offstage after I'd faked my orgasm, carried me into an elevator and then into a dark, spacious suite of rooms at the very top of the building. He'd laid me on a bed covered in black silk and rubbed something cold and slick on my ass and my back, and then he'd handed me fresh panties.

When I'd stared at them dazedly, not moving to change, he'd peeled off my old ones and then worked the fresh pair over my hips. I had been sat up like a doll, my hair brushed, and then a glass of water held to my lips.

I had sipped, looking down at where Mark knelt in front of me, holding the glass.

"Thank you, sir," I'd managed to mumble, and that thing had moved behind his eyes again.

He hadn't told me that we didn't have to pretend when we

were alone; he hadn't reminded me that what had happened on the stage was all an illusion.

Instead, he'd wrapped me in a soft blanket and carried me back downstairs, where I had sat cuddled and warm in his lap the rest of the night. And despite the music, the noise, and the carnal displays happening on the stage, I had fallen fast asleep.

When I had woken up, I had woken up alone in my hotel room, with a tube of arnica gel, a bottle of ibuprofen, and several bottles of water to greet me.

The flight to Rome had been miserable with an ass that raw.

I hadn't seen Mark since. And I was fine with that, I reasoned. We'd pulled off our little act convincingly. No doubt in anyone's mind that I was the type Mark could conceivably choose to marry. It didn't matter what I'd felt on stage and what I'd felt curled up in his lap after. That was irrelevant. Unnecessary. Sinful, even.

But then again, I was full of sins these days. New sins on behalf of the Church. Sins that made anything I did with Mark practically moral in comparison.

A whole sacrifice, my uncle had told me while I was in Rome. *A burnt offering. The pain you feel over your sins to save God's kingdom will be sweeter than incense.*

I wondered if anyone else could smell the smoke coming off me, or if it was only God.

Preoccupied, I stepped out of the car when it stopped and the door was opened for me, slinging my leather backpack over my shoulder as I walked into my building. I was grateful for college because it gave me something else to focus on, to fill up my thoughts and hours, so that after a day of training, praying, studying, I was too exhausted to think of this last summer. To think of Lyonesse and Rome.

Both had been baptisms, in a way. Both had been confirmations too, but with pounding blood and fevered adrenaline instead of oil and communion.

I looked down at my hands as the doorman summoned the private elevator for me and I stepped inside. I wasn't sure what I expected to see; they were still my hands. When I looked in the mirror, it was still my face.

Despite what had happened in Rome, I was still Isolde Laurence.

Happened. That word. Like I'd had no choice, like it was all something that had fallen into my lap. What had happened this summer was hardly that; I had chosen it all, every step of the way.

Your sins to save God's kingdom.

The elevator doors slid open, and I stepped into the open expanse of the great room, already thinking I would grab something easy to eat and then spend the rest of the evening working on a paper for my pre-Columbian art class. My father was in London, Bryn was back at Wellesley, and I was alone.

Something I was a lot, it seemed.

But I'd only made it a single step into the penthouse before something tingled at the back of my neck.

Someone was here.

Silently, I bent down to unlace my boots and pull them from my feet. I slid my bag to the floor, pulling the knife with the honeysuckle blade from the front pocket and easing it from its black leather sheath as I crept toward the grand spiral staircase that led up to the library and then to the observatory. Someone was up there, I was certain of it, and it wasn't my father, and it wouldn't be cleaning staff at this time of day. The building was supposedly secure, but as I'd learned in Rome, that hardly mattered to someone with the right motivation.

I mounted the stairs in my bare feet, moving the knife from standard grip to reverse grip as I did, like Mark had shown me in the karate school more than two years ago. It had felt so foreign in my hand then, random and awkward, my movements random and awkward with it. Now—after years of being determined never to be bested like Mark had bested me that day—I felt certain and assured with any knife I happened to pick up, and especially with this one. The way Mark had it made was indelible perfection: sometimes my hand felt wrong *without* the bone and gold handle nestled in my palm, rather than the other way around.

The bone was warm in my hand as the library came into view. Shelves and shelves of books collected over the years— my mother's favorite books about medicine, chemistry, and botany, books Uncle Mortimer had sent from Rome written in all the languages I'd been made to learn as a girl. Even my father's pretentious collection of leather-bound antiques, purchased for decoration, looked organic and at home with all the other titles.

Twenty-two windows lit the circular space, revealing the fading autumn light, and a massive globe gleamed next to two armchairs. It was open, and a decanter of whisky sat unstoppered inside it.

But that wasn't what had caught my attention. At the far window, looking out toward the Hudson, was a man in a charcoal gray suit, a tumbler of my father's favorite single malt dangling from his fingers. Even though it was late in the day, the suit was still immaculately pressed and his blond hair was styled perfectly in place.

"Going to kill me, Isolde?" asked Mark as I climbed the final step. He hadn't turned around to look at me, so how—

The window. He could see my reflection in the window, knife and all. A rookie mistake—something that happened all too often around him.

I didn't sheath the knife or put it away, however.

"How did you get inside?" I asked warily.

He still didn't turn, merely lifting a shoulder and then raising the glass to his mouth. "I have my ways."

Bribing the doorman, most likely. I'd have to look into that later. I could no longer afford the presumption that any space was completely secure. "*Why* are you here? If you wanted to arrange another training session or appearance at Lyonesse, you could have texted—"

"Have you spoken to your father recently?" Mark interrupted.

My father? "No. He's in London right now."

Mark took a drink and then braced his forearm on the window as he swallowed. "He spoke to me today. About our engagement."

A thousand different possibilities swarmed through my mind.

Did Father want to end this betrothal, after being the one to force me into it in the first place? What would Uncle Mortimer think? And would it mean I could return to my original plan of taking vows after college?

Surprisingly, the thought didn't bring the relief it might have once, nor the joy. I still wanted to live as a nun, of course; it was the dream that had been snatched from me—but—

But I didn't know. Maybe I'd adapted too much to the idea of being joined to the cold, suited man in front of me. Or maybe I'd seen too much, done too much, to imagine myself as a bride of Christ now. I'd already begun creating a life as Christ's mistress instead, seeking his love from the shadows rather than the light.

And perhaps it was the role I'd been shaped for anyway. Gathering crumbs for my uncle among the world's elite, turning my body into a weapon…all of that would hardly be useful in a cloister, and I wanted to be useful above all. To *serve* God, not just with my prayers, but my hands too. And for better or for worse, *serving* was inextricably threaded with marrying the man across the room.

"And what did he say?" I asked. My voice was steady, even, though I felt anything but steady right now.

"He said"—Mark's voice was rough and bitter, and there was heat in it. I wondered how much scotch he'd drunk—"he'd like some surety that we are following through with our engagement, and that our marriage is inevitable."

"Surety," I repeated. I had no idea what my father could mean. The prenuptial agreements had long signed and filed away, and now that my graduation was only two and a half years away, there had already been some talk about hiring a wedding planner. As far as I knew, everything was happening as it was meant to.

Mark took another drink, dropped his arm from the glass. "This is the first you've heard of it, then?"

"I have no idea what you or my father are talking about." Which I hated. It was never a good idea to be in the dark when it came to either of those men.

Mark finally turned to face me. Those sculpted lips were curled in an expression so disgusted that I would have taken a step backward if I weren't still so close to the stairs.

"Well, then let me enlighten you." The words were as hard as the look in his eyes. "Your father would like for me to deflower you. The sooner the better, in his mind."

I stared at him.

The words didn't fit together, didn't make any kind of sense. And I don't mean that in a metaphorical way—they genuinely made no sense to me.

Deflower.

The sooner the better.

Mark didn't move or speak as his words finally, painfully, transformed into meaning—as my lips parted and my chest lifted in a sharp breath.

My father wanted Mark to fuck me.

It was so medieval that I almost couldn't ascribe it to my iPad-wielding, Savile Row-clad father.

…Almost.

But—

"Why?" I whispered. "Why does it matter?"

Mark didn't speak as I stepped away from the stairs, turning to face the desk in the corner of the room. My father worked in here sometimes when he was in Manhattan; Mother and I used to run up the stairs as fast as we could and try to jump in his lap. He'd act surprised and then tickle us both until we were shrieking.

And now I was staring at that same desk as I stood across from the man who'd bought me in marriage, whom my father had apparently told to claim my virginity like some kind of trophy.

Did he think Mark needed further incentive to marry me beyond what had already been agreed on? Did he think Mark was so easily won over? Mark had an entire club of people to fuck, and I didn't doubt that he was fucking people outside of it too. One college student's hymen was hardly going to tip the scales in either direction.

"He must know—he has to know that you'd have no remorse over this. That it won't trap you into going through with the wedding if you decide you don't want to marry me."

I turned in time to see Mark's jaw work to the side. "It's not me he wants to trap, Isolde," he said after a moment.

"But if he doesn't want to trap you, then who does he—" I stopped, my breath catching. "Oh."

"Yes," Mark said. "*Oh*."

My father wanted to trap me instead. Whether it was because he believed me secretly romantic and naïve, or because he wanted to manipulate my Catholic morality, I couldn't be sure, but it didn't matter. My father believed that if I had sex with Mark, I'd feel compelled to marry him.

It was insurance against my potential resistance.

Anger punched at my lungs, and I had to fight to keep my breath regular in front of the too-perceptive Mark.

But how could my father do this? When I'd already been so compliant, so *fucking* obedient, even when it came to giving up the life I'd always wanted?

"Bold of him to assume I've never had sex," I muttered.

Mark gave a short nod.

"Not that I…what we did on the stage at Lyonesse—that was the closest anyone's ever come to touching me—" I stopped, flushed. "I presume you told him that he had no right to ask such a thing?"

"I told him that I would do with my future wife whatever I damn well wished," Mark said flatly. The words were just as medieval as my father's demands, but I didn't feel a renewed rush of anger at hearing them.

I also didn't care to look too closely at what it was that I *did* feel.

"And what did he say to that?"

Mark lifted his glass to his lips but didn't take a drink. "That he was prepared to make it an essential condition of our engagement. He doesn't trust that you won't be seduced back to God otherwise."

An essential condition.

"So he would…what? Cancel the engagement if we don't comply?"

Mark responded without inflection.

"Yes."

That didn't make any kind of sense! My father had been the one to demand this marriage—and now like a petulant child, he was saying he'd stop it from happening at all? If we didn't give into his horrific demands?

"He's minimizing risk," observed Mark over his glass. "It's what bankers do. If he can't be certain the marriage will happen, he needs to know in enough time to dampen the

127

embarrassment, to control the narrative. And potentially to position you for another alliance."

I had to admit that all sounded like my father.

But maybe…maybe this was it. My opening, my chance—a door left cracked by my father's arrogance. Whether it was because he was that confident he'd bend us to his will, or because he was so stubborn that he'd see this arrangement dissolved if it couldn't be sealed in blood, I didn't know. But what did it matter, actually?

What did it actually matter?

I'd never chosen this for my father. I'd chosen it for Mortimer and for my church; I'd chosen it for *me*. How funny that Father was afraid I'd renege on the engagement because of my faith…when I'd agreed to be scourged by marriage because of that very same faith.

And perhaps if my father knew the truth, we wouldn't be here in this moment; he'd be secure in knowing that I was fully committed. But there was no way for him to know the truth without also revealing how Uncle Mortimer wanted to leverage the alliance with Mark, and there was no way to explain *that* without my loyalties becoming clear.

And it served no one for my father to learn that any loyalty to him ranked very, very low on a list of my motivations.

So the engagement couldn't end. I'd come too far, changed too much, for that.

I closed my eyes and thought through our remaining options. If my father had gone so far as to speak to Mark about this, then he was determined to have it. In a battle of wills with Geoffrey Laurence, Mark Trevena very well might win—and so might I, although I never had before. But I had also learned a great many things from my uncle, and one of them was that pride should never come at the price of expediency.

"So we lie." I opened my eyes to see Mark watching me.

He still had the glass held up to his mouth, like he couldn't decide whether to take a drink. "You tell him that we've had sex, and that my Catholic guilt has led me into a deep emotional attachment to you, and that you're confident I'll go through with the marriage."

"You should know that your father has intimated to me that he's already bribed your physician to keep him abreast of any physical changes. Or the lack thereof."

Fresh horror washed through me. Pure, unwashed horror at the intrusion, the violation of it.

The *evil* of it.

My own father, the same father who'd sat on a kitchen counter and kicked his feet while he allowed my mother to feed him her culinary disasters—the same father who'd never missed a school concert, a teacher's meeting, a chance to swing me on his shoulders—had done this. To me, his only child.

Had my mother's death truly changed him that much? Or had it been my mother keeping him good all those years, and then after her funeral, he'd reverted to whatever reptilian being he'd been before he met her?

Mark drained the rest of the scotch in a practiced swallow. "I can, of course, out-bribe your father," he said as he walked over to the open globe again. "And you can change doctors. We can select one known for privacy and discretion; we can make sure they are properly bribed or blackmailed too."

Mark used the word *blackmail* so easily, so casually, that it startled me. I didn't know why—what else was all that information he collected good for?

"But," he went on as he poured himself more single malt, "we will have to contend with the possibility that we might be outmaneuvered at some point. He might flip someone loyal to us if he's able to access the right leverage, or offer more money before I can counter. It's a risk we have to take, but I anticipate we can minimize it as much as possible—"

"Wait," I said, and then stopped, unsure of what I was going to say next.

He raised an eyebrow, thick and straight and a dark gold, nearly the same color as the drink in his glass. "Yes?"

"I—" I took a breath. "What are our other options?"

"There are no other options, sweetheart. We can lie and wait to be found out—or we can lie and blackmail someone into lying along with us."

Sweetheart.

It was the first time he'd called me such a thing. Heat threatened to bloom on my cheeks; my heart was thudding. I had to force myself to think again.

Pride couldn't come at the cost of expediency. And hadn't I already expected something like this? Hadn't I already anticipated that Mark would have sex with me? I'd intentionally given the green light when it came to my limits, after all, and after New Year's Eve and what had happened on stage at Lyonesse, I had to admit that I wanted it.

I wanted to have sex with him.

And anyway, it was necessary for bringing Mark closer to me, for earning his trust and affection and anything else I could use to squeeze all the blood out of this marriage that I could.

Your sins to save God's kingdom.

"There is one other option," I said. Calmly. "You could deflower me for real."

thirteen

He didn't react at first, other than a single muscle jumping along the side of his jaw.

"No," he said finally, and stepped away from the globe.

"No?"

"Absolutely not," he clarified. "I have many kinks, but acrimonious regret isn't one of them."

I studied him. "Why would you regret it?"

He sighed, closing his eyes, and once again, I wondered how much he'd had to drink. This was the most expressive I'd ever seen him, and it was captivating to watch. Like watching the waters of a cold, deep lake recede to reveal a drowned village.

"I'm not talking about myself, Isolde." He opened his eyes and met my stare with a hard, dangerous one of his own. "I mean *you*. You would regret it."

"I wouldn't," I said—although even as I said it, I wondered.

Would I? Would there always be an invisible Isolde in my head, one untouched by her father and uncle's schemes, who'd been able to choose differently?

But you can't choose differently. I'd taken this road with my eyes wide open; I'd anticipated having sex with Mark eventually, had chosen it. My virginity would be just another offering laid down on the altar, ready to burn, and I'd finally accepted that I was eager to strike the match.

Mark clearly didn't believe me, given the skeptical set of his mouth, and I stepped forward.

"I wouldn't regret it," I said again. "It's something I assumed would happen eventually."

"*Eventually* is very different from right now."

"And," I went on, "it doesn't matter, does it? Virginity? I thought you of all people would feel that way."

Mark gave me a look. "Do you want me to tell you that your hymen is just like tonsils or an appendix? That removing it together would be clinical and unremarkable?"

"Well, not unremarkable, necessarily, but the concept of—"

"I'm well aware of the bullshit premise of virginity, Isolde. It's also permissible for it to matter to you, or to me."

"*Does* it matter to you?" I asked. He'd never intimated that it did; he'd been explicit about fidelity after our wedding but had never mentioned if he expected me to wear white honestly on our wedding day.

Mark's eyes flicked down to his glass and then back up to me. It was momentary, brief. I could almost convince myself that I'd imagined it.

"Divided loyalty matters to me," he said. His voice was firm, convincing. "If you come to hate me later because of this, that is a problem. If this is the seed of some future discontent, that is also a problem. This arrangement only makes sense if I can count on us being united after our marriage."

"No perceived gap between us, I remember." I stepped closer again, near the globe now. "But I don't think you answered the question I asked. Does me being a virgin—or staying a virgin—matter to you?"

"If you're asking whether my estimation of you is contingent on you possessing a hymen, then the answer is no."

"And if I'm asking something else?"

That muscle in his jaw jumped again, and then he lifted the scotch to his lips and took a long drink. He took his time before replying. "And what are you asking, sweetheart?"

I didn't know what I was asking. I didn't know what it was that I wanted him to say. I wanted my virginity not to matter to him, because then we could dampen the fires of my father's suspicion in the most efficient way. I wanted my virginity to matter to him because I wanted it to matter to someone, this physical marker of my choices.

Maybe *I* wanted to matter to someone. Even if it was only through the lens of sex. I wanted to be something more than a tool, a means to an end.

Or maybe you just want more of what Mark gave you at Lyonesse.

His flogger raining hellfire on my skin. His hand on my throat while the other searched between my legs. I could tell myself it was for my own purposes, for my long game of winning him over to me, but the truth was evident in the stiff ache of my nipples, the swollen pulse at the apex of my sex.

I wanted him beyond the wisdom of a seduction—a humiliating thing, especially given that he'd made no effort whatsoever to seduce me. In fact, he'd been enormously careful not to take advantage of the unusual nature of our meetings. It spoke to his twisted sense of morality, maybe, but it stung my pride too. I knew I wasn't flirtatious or sultry—I knew that I carried myself like a curled fist. That didn't mean I didn't want to be desired as I myself desired him.

And anyway, he wasn't supposed to have any morality, twisted or not. He was supposed to be a devil.

Why wouldn't he be *my* devil, then?

I lifted my chin. I couldn't help my pride, but I could help my honesty.

"Do you want to deflower me, Mark?"

His jaw worked to the side as he looked down at his glass again. Then he set it down on the small shelf inside the globe.

Sensing that I was getting to him, I stepped closer. Closer again. "Is that a hard limit for you? Virgin brides?"

"Isolde." He said my name like a warning.

"There's no difference to me between it happening now or on our wedding night."

"Stop," he said sharply, but I didn't stop. This close to him, I could see that his pupils were dilated, that there was the faintest flush to his cheeks.

From the scotch? Or something else?

I remembered how it had felt to hear his breathing change the first time I'd crawled to him; how his erection felt pressed against me. Even if it was only convenient or casual desire, he *did* desire me.

I asked for you.

I wanted you.

And despite the fourteen years between us, despite all his power and money and violence, I pushed.

"So let's do it. There's nothing to be negotiated, nothing to be discussed. I am willing, and unless you aren't—"

"That is not the problem," he said tightly.

"Then what is?" I stepped closer again, close enough that I could see the pulse in his throat, my reflection in his onyx eyes. "Why won't you tell me? I'm being honest with you—"

And just like that, he moved. I was faster than I'd been two years ago, and so I almost evaded him, but he was still quicker, stronger. He had his hand around my jaw, tipping my face up to his, and his other hand wrapped tightly around my wrist. To control the hand that held the knife. I'd forgotten I was holding it.

"I promise that you do not want my honesty in return.

Out of respect for the difference in our ages and the circumstances of our connection, I have kept a curtain between us," he said. His voice held so much malice and anger in it that it was terrifying to hear, and his fingers were so tight on my jaw that they almost hurt. A thrill raced down my spine. "You don't want to be on the other side of that curtain."

"I think I do," I whispered.

"You do not," he said. "Because on the other side of the curtain is being mine. Belonging to *me*, and I do not mean the version of myself that I've allowed you to see. I do not mean the careful, thoughtful man that you believe that I am. I've fostered that belief—fed it as much as I could—because I do regret that your future had to be sacrificed for my gain, and it will make the next handful of years go easier for us both. But you do not want to test me on this, darling. Stay on the other side where it's safe."

"Or what?" The words came out tight, almost whispered, with his fingers holding my jaw like they were.

"Or you will learn why people whisper my name," he said, the words as rough as his fingers on my skin. "Why I've never collared a submissive. What it looks like when I decide to have someone as my own."

He lowered his mouth to my ear and murmured, "There would be no politeness, no mercy. Your only recourse would be your safe word. I've waited years to have someone belong to me, and I would make you feel every day, every hour, that I've abstained."

He pulled back, his eyes boring into mine. There was only a thin ring of blue around the black. "Do you understand? You do not want this. Let's go back to being polite accomplices in an arranged marriage, actors playing our parts, and we will find some other way around your father's suspicions. You'll thank me later."

"No." I tried to step forward into him, but couldn't, not

with the hands on my jaw and wrist. "I won't. I want it. Don't you want it? Don't you want me?"

He leaned in, dragging his nose through my hair. I shivered.

"I am *all* want with you, Isolde. You think that I don't think about you all the time? That I don't want your scent all over my bed? You think that I don't wish I had you under my desk with that serious little mouth available for my relief every morning? That I don't want your snug cunt whenever I goddamn feel like it? Yes, I want you, and I want you collared, and I want you mine. That should be enough to terrify you, because I would hold nothing back until I'd eaten your very soul. I would hold nothing back until it was written on your skin and scratched into your bones how much I crave you."

I couldn't breathe for the thudding of my heart, the slick, needy heat throbbing in my sex. His words were something more than words, some kind of prayer or invocation, some kind of spell, conjuring between us what I had thought was only contained to my dreams. To my darkest and most secret fantasies.

And he *wanted me*. He wanted me with ferocity, with teeth and bruising greed, and he wanted me to be shockingly, perilously *his*.

Oh, how I yearned for that. To belong to this brutal devil, to surrender to him. I would never be lonely, never feel unwanted. Never wake up and feel like purpose or service was forever out of reach, because it would be as easy as breathing, as surrendering to him.

I stared up at him, dazed and hungry, my eyes caught by his own.

"And you think your virginity is a hard limit for me?" His laugh was carnivorous. "It wouldn't have changed my fascination with you one bit if you weren't a virgin, just so you're aware. But you'd better believe I've thought about nothing else since you agreed to marry me. Nothing but that pretty little cunt, the one that comes just from being punished. How tight it would be, how swollen and slick I could make it before I wedged my way inside." He bent his mouth to mine, hovering just above my lips, his breath tickling me. "Knowing I was the first person there, the first person to taste it and the first person to fill it. The first person to stretch you to take someone."

"Then have it," I whispered. "It's yours."

"I like that word on your tongue," Mark murmured, his lips now ghosting over mine as he spoke. "*Yours*. I want to taste it there."

"Then do it," I begged. I was breathless, desperate. All my plans and strategies erased by the simmering lust crawling through my veins.

No. Not just lust. I didn't know what to call it, but this was something else, something worse. It was like my soul needed to be fucked as much as my body did, and what that meant about me, about God, I didn't know. I just knew that I wasn't going to survive the next few minutes if Mark didn't kiss me, didn't take me.

I wanted to be on the other side of that curtain more than I'd wanted anything else ever in my life—and *that* was the most terrifying thing of all.

His tongue traced along my parted lips, dipping inside just enough to lick along the edges of my teeth.

"Please, sir," I whimpered, not even recognizing my own voice, myself. The *sir* that spilled out as naturally as an exhale. "Make me yours. I'll be so good for you; I'll be yours as long as you want—"

His mouth sealed over mine and claimed it. His fingers held my jaw still as his tongue searched out mine and licked, as if he were truly trying to taste the word I'd spoken that he'd liked so much. *Yours*. Like he could lap it up like wine.

I moaned into the kiss, my skin tight and hot and my pulse kicking everywhere, like I was in a fight, and I needed more and more and more. He nipped at my lower lip, swallowing my gasp, as his other hand took the knife from me and set it next to his scotch.

"I'm glad you like your present, my deadly girl," he said against my mouth. "Now tell me you remember your safe word."

"Hyssop." It sounded like a plea—not to stop, but to keep going. "I'll say it if I need it, I promise."

His hand found my hair and threaded through the tresses, and he pulled my head back so that he could look at my face.

"You," he said, his other hand finding the hem of my respectable skirt and shoving it up to my waist, "are a terrible idea."

He looked down at where my white cotton panties were exposed and let out a sharp, ragged exhale. "So maybe it's fitting that I'm a terrible idea too."

That felt more right than any endearment, any declaration. He was using me to build his empire, and I was using him to build God's, and somewhere along the way, we'd both come to need whatever this was. However depraved, however wrong, however stupid. We needed it like fire needed oxygen, and now we were burning together.

He let go of my hair and then hauled me up into his arms, carrying me over to the desk and setting me down on the edge. He stepped back and began unbuttoning his suit jacket.

"Spread your legs," he said, his voice brooking no argument. "And pull your skirt back up. I need to see it."

There was no mistaking which *it* he meant—the object of his obsession. And when I obeyed, the breath that shuddered out of him was worth every agony leading up to this moment, worth every sin and every shame.

"Pull your panties to the side," he ordered, now stripping off his jacket and tossing it carelessly over the back of a nearby chair. Without it, I could see the impressive tent in his suit trousers. "Hold them there until I've looked my fill."

I quivered as my fingers dropped against my thigh, I was that worked up. And when I curled my fingers around the cotton, I could feel how damp I'd made everything down there. Given the first shiver of cool air over my cunt, I knew it was wet enough to *look* wet, and sure enough, Mark gave a punched breath at the sight.

"So pretty," he said and pressed the heel of his palm to his erection. "So, so pretty."

He came closer and then knelt on one knee, like a man preparing to propose. Except his ring was already on my finger, and he wasn't giving any romantic speeches. Instead, he was using his thumbs to brush lightly over the softness of my vulva, using them to spread me apart so that he could look inside.

His nostrils flared, and his jaw was rigid. He almost looked furious: dilated eyes and the parted, hungry lips. "It's a very good thing I didn't see this until now," he told me, not taking his eyes off my pussy. "A good thing for both of us."

He bent in, and without warning, pressed a long, open kiss to it.

My thighs tried to shut; my hips squirmed. It was hot and ticklish and slick, and nothing like I'd ever felt before, ever, ever. Not with my fingers, not with the corner of my mattress, not even in my dreams, because I hadn't known to dream about this. And when his tongue flicked over my clitoris, my head fell back as I panted.

"How does that feel?" he asked, not lifting his head from my cunt.

"So good," I groaned. "Like you're licking my heart."

"I would if I could," said Mark in a voice full of dark promise. He gave me another long kiss, sucking the swollen pearl between his lips before releasing it and swirling his tongue inside my opening, making noises of rough pleasure as he did.

He stood up and then kissed me, forcing me to sample myself on his lips. Sweet and strange, a taste unlike any other.

"I needed to taste it," he said as he pulled back to look at my cunt again. "My brand-new toy. Now open for me." He slid his first two fingers into my mouth, and instinctively, I closed my lips around them and sucked. His eyes darkened even more.

"Good girl," he said, and a hot, fierce pleasure curled in my chest.

Then he dropped his fingers between my legs, his eyes back down to my pussy. To where he was slowly parting me, finding the tight entrance between my folds.

"Wait," I said, and he shook his head.

"That's not how it works between us," he murmured, dropping his lips to my jaw and then my mouth. "My deadly girl, my little honeysuckle queen. Say *hyssop* to me, and I'll stop the instant you say it. But I won't break for *wait*, not for *stop*. Not even for *no*. Your safe word is all of those things, and more. It's your freedom and your power too."

"But don't you—" His wet fingertips were still searching me out, and then one made a lazy circle just outside my entrance. "Don't you want to put your cock there instead? Sir?"

He froze, and then shuddered out a exhale against my mouth.

"Yes, I want to put my cock there, Isolde. More than anything. But let's not test my control too far yet, hmm?"

As he said it, he was already straightening up, his eyes dropping to his hand. "This will pinch," he warned, and I fought to breathe as his finger pressed deeper.

His expression was avid, awed—gleeful—as he watched his thick finger penetrate me. Taking something that shouldn't matter, that didn't matter—and yet also did, because we'd decided together that it meant something. That it was his to have, even if it didn't change anything about what came next.

And then the pain, a sharp, low agony that had me panting and squirming.

"That's it," Mark said, still in that voice full of dark promise. "Just a minute longer." His free hand came to wrap around my hip and hold me still as he tore me between the legs. And just when I thought I couldn't stand it for a second longer, he added a second finger.

I made a low, whining noise then, the pain clawing up to my chest and my throat, stealing my air. It was clean and gorgeous and awakening, like all the torment he gave me.

Not for a second did I think about saying my safe word.

"So tight, Isolde," Mark praised. "So good to take what I give you, even when it hurts. Keep those legs spread for me. Let me see that pretty pussy getting filled for the first time."

The pain was shimmering in me now, settling into my bones, and when I looked down, I saw blood, slick and red, covering his fingers.

He looked up and met my eyes, and a sadistic smile stretched that beautiful mouth of his. His eyes were large and black and fringed with gold lashes, and his muscled shoulder and bicep were moving under his shirt as he worked his big fingers in and out of my virgin hole, and how had I ever thought he wasn't handsome? That his angular jaw and sculpted cheeks weren't geometric perfection? That the bump in his nose and the scar near his temple weren't dangerously beautiful?

That his smile wouldn't put the devil's to shame?

"You take me so gorgeously," he murmured. "After we're married and you come to live with me, you'll take my cock every night. Every day. As often as I need, and I need it a lot, Isolde. I'll need your mouth and cunt and eventually your ass too, and you'll be my pet, my little wife, to give me relief."

I moaned, the shimmering pain pulling at my lungs, my

funny bones, but at my pussy too. His grin stretched even wider. "Oh, I felt that little quiver, sweetheart. Can you come with your blood all over my hand? Show me. Show me how much you like being mine."

He pressed his thumb to the erect bud above my entrance and began working it, just as his fingers worked in and out of my channel, their entry made slick and wet by arousal and blood. I let out a choked groan as pleasure yanked abruptly between my legs, brought on by his expert touch, by the need evident in the hard cock straining his pants and in the hungry lines of his face.

"I want to come," I mumbled, my head dropping forward into his shoulder. "I want to come, I want to come, I want—"

The pleasure detonated so fast that my breath stilled and my back bowed and my mouth parted in a silent, choked scream as the convulsions tore their way up my body, from my throbbing clitoris to my womb to my chest, robbing me of air and thought and anything that wasn't filthy, mindless pleasure. I came around Mark's fingers, squeezing them, using them, my hips bucking as if trying to fuck them deeper and harder into me.

He watched with undisguised enjoyment as I futilely tried to spear my cunt on his fingers, and then as I slowly, slowly went still, shivering and whimpering and limp.

He pressed his hand to my sternum and pushed me backward, so I was laying on my back lengthwise across the desk.

"What are you doing?" I said in a dizzy, sated voice, but I had my answer soon enough. After pulling my blood-spattered underwear from my hips—and then shoving them in his back pocket—he unzipped his pants and freed his stiff organ.

I'd never seen one in person before. It was circumcised and thick and straight, long enough that his hand had to travel some distance as he gave himself a few leisurely pumps. A thick vein meandered up the side, and the head was flared and swollen.

It was shiny and wet at the tip, like it had been leaking for some time in his pants.

Mark swiped his hand over my pussy, and I wondered for a moment what he was doing, until he returned the same hand to his cock and began masturbating with short, vicious strokes.

He was using the blood from my hymen and the slickness of my pleasure as lube.

With my panties gone and my skirt shoved up to my hips, there was nothing between him and my bare cunt. His eyes trailed over it as the muscles in his shoulder and arm flexed while he worked himself. My body stirred again just to see it.

His hand was tight, unrelenting on himself, and I saw something of his lust then, of how worked up he was, of how deep the need must claw at him, because he jerked himself like he would murder someone just to come. Just to feel relief from whatever lashed and bit at him in his thoughts.

The skin of his cock was stretched tight and slicked with red and his fist was huge and strong, and then with a satisfied noise that curled my toes, he gave himself a series of fast strokes and jetted thick stripes of semen onto my sex.

It was so much, hot and dripping, and he kept pumping himself with rough motions until he was done. When he let go of his cock, he was still half-hard, and he drew lazy fingers up the mess he'd made. He pressed the messy fingers to my mouth, and I opened automatically, sucking them clean.

"What a good wife you'll make," he rasped, bending over me to give me a long, possessive kiss. His scent—like the city after a storm—was all around me, now the air I breathed. "What a perfect queen, with her honeysuckle knife and her sweet cunt."

My skin was tingling, my vision flickering with static. If I wasn't already flat on my back, I would have fallen over. It was like the first time I'd crawled to him, the first time he'd cuffed me to his cross. Like the entire world was buzzing under my skin.

Like I'd float right up to the stars if he let me.

He straightened up, finding a handkerchief from somewhere and using it to wipe me clean of blood and semen. My pussy was inspected once again, this time with satisfaction stamped all over his face, and then I was up in his arms, being carried somewhere. My bedroom, I realized at the same time that I also realized my delirium was edging into sleepiness.

Mark knew where my bedroom was. The thought didn't unnerve me the way it should have. The way it would have if I were thinking straight.

I was stripped of my clothes, given ibuprofen and water, and settled in bed. More water was set on my bedside table, and just when I thought he was going to leave, he sat on the edge of the bed and pushed my hair behind my ear. He didn't speak, content to stroke my head while I closed my eyes and rested.

"How do you feel?" he asked. It was strange to hear his voice filled with heat, with naked interest.

I loved it.

"My pussy hurts," I murmured honestly. "And I feel amazing. Are you going to leave?"

He didn't speak for a moment, and when I opened my eyes to look up at him, I found his eyes fixed on my hair. On where he rubbed the silky tresses between his fingertips.

"I'd like to stay," he said finally. "I don't know how advisable it is, but I'd like to stay."

"Thank you." I closed my eyes again. "I wish I hurt more so that you'd have to do more aftercare."

"Aftercare is more than pain management, Isolde," he said. "What would you like?"

"I don't know," I said, still dizzy and tingling. Endorphins, maybe. I was high on them. "I just want you with me."

I heard a soft thud, and then a second thud. His shoes

being toed off. And then he crawled onto the mattress, coming to rest behind me with my back to his chest and my bottom tucked snugly against his lap. His clothes were the kind of expensive that felt amazing to rub and snuggle against.

He was huge in my bed, tall and wide and muscular, radiating heat. I turned in his arms and nuzzled my face against him, which seemed to surprise him. But then he wrapped his arms around me and pulled me closer.

"What happens next?" I mumbled, sleep already pulling me under. "Sir?"

He let out a long exhale. He liked it when I said *sir*. "I figure out what to do with you, sweetheart. That's what happens next."

I couldn't believe that Mark Trevena was here in my bed, holding me. But he was, and it felt perfect, even with my sore pussy throbbing between my legs. And I didn't have a single regret about anything.

I'd do it again in a heartbeat.

Tomorrow would begin a new chapter for us. I would be his in all the ways he'd tried to warn me away from, and maybe, just maybe, a tiny piece of this cold, deadly, hungry man would also be mine.

fourteen

It wasn't yet dawn when I woke.

I opened my eyes to a room lit only by the glow of the city, my room a chiaroscuro of gold and shadow. Mark stood by my window, his suit jacket and shoes back on, not a hair out of place. His eyes were on the glass, and something flipped between his fingers as he stared at the still-sleeping city.

I sat up, the sheet falling from my naked body. Even though it was still dark outside, it was close to when I'd wake up to pray anyway, and I didn't feel tired in the least. Possibly because I'd fallen asleep much earlier than normal. Possibly because Mark was still here. Mark was here, and last night had happened, and everything had changed.

"You're awake," he said. "Good."

He turned toward me, setting whatever it was he'd been twirling between his fingers on my desk.

I watched him, not bothering to cover myself, enjoying the way his dark gaze dripped over my collarbone and exposed breasts before coming back to my face.

"How are you feeling?" he asked.

I stretched a little to test my body, noticing that his gaze followed my movements, and then I smiled a little as I felt the twinge inside me. What had hurt last night felt like a token this morning, a sweet memory. Proof that Mark had let me on the other side of his curtain. "I'm a little sore, but that's all."

I had no idea how to seduce him into more of what we had done last night, no idea how to even begin asking for it. But I wanted it. I wanted him to stride to my bed and put his hand between my legs. I wanted him to use me to get off again. I wanted—I wanted *him*. Us. I wanted this breathless ache in my chest to ease.

"Good," he said. "You didn't sleep well, so I was worried."

"I slept better than I have in a long time," I said. It was the truth. Ever since my trip to Rome this summer, nightmares had awaited me every time I closed my eyes.

My honeysuckle knife flashing in the dark; blood wet and coppery on my face. My uncle laying his hand on my gore-crusted hair in the already hot morning sunshine of Rome.

Your sins to save God's kingdom.

But the dreams had been muffled last night, blurry. Unable to hurt me in Mark's strong, possessive embrace.

Mark stepped closer without speaking, and I squinted to read his expression. It was impossible in this light, with his cheekbones and jaw lit in gold and his mouth and eyes partially draped in shadow. I thought of his face last night as he'd put his fingers inside me, as he'd come all over my cunt.

What a good little wife you'll make.

"So did you figure it out?" I asked. I was unable to stop the excitement blooming in my chest. I was his. I'd fought it for the last two years, resisting him, resisting the way he made me feel, the way crawling and being bound and held and flogged had made me feel, but no longer.

I was his.

"Figure what out?" he asked. His voice was cold again, polite. Nothing like it had been just hours ago.

I should have known then, I think. That something had changed. But I was nineteen, feeling the first flush of submission and sex and love, and I didn't want to know anything that wasn't this heady, delirious thrill.

"What to do with me," I prompted, dropping my legs over the side of the bed to stand. "What happens next."

Mark regarded me as I stood, not moving. Him dressed, suited, and me utterly naked.

"I have," he said calmly.

"And?"

"And," he said, stepping forward, "we won't need to meet again until the wedding."

A new buzz started under my skin, but it was one of alarm. Just like before, my body knew before my mind did.

"Sorry?" I whispered.

"We've done a commendable job of selling our engagement as real so far, and we've now ensured your father has no reason to doubt you. There's no reason for us to see each other until the wedding, unless, of course, we decide to present the illusion that I've collared you. We'll need to make something of the collaring, a little ceremony at the club, but I'll make sure it's brief and to the point."

"Illusion," I said.

Yes, I want you, and I want you collared, and I want you mine. That should be enough to terrify you, because I would hold nothing back until I'd eaten your very heart.

I still couldn't make out Mark's expression, not enough of it, at least. All I could see was that sculpted mouth in the shape of utter indifference. His eyes glittering from the shadows.

"I don't understand," I said. The words were bitter on my tongue, and I knew it was because they tasted like failure, like defeat.

Even now, I refuse to admit to myself that they tasted like heartbreak.

"I think you do understand," Mark said. He had a hand in his pocket as he looked at me. "I think you understand what's happening very well."

"But you said—" I stopped. I sounded childish. Pleading for a grown-up not to leave her alone in the dark.

Mark had lied last night. About wanting me to be his—possibly about all of it. His body hadn't lied, but that didn't matter. He'd used my body as a tool against me, and undoubtedly, he could use his own body as a tool when necessary. Same as a flogger or a pair of leather cuffs, his hands and his cock were just part of a scene. Even when that scene was entirely a lie.

I closed my eyes, shame dripping into my gut. Hot and viscous.

I'd believed him last night. I'd believed every word he said about wanting me, about keeping distance between us in order to keep me safe. Because I'd wanted to hear it. I'd wanted him to want me as much as I wanted him; I'd wanted him to give me no choice about being his.

I wanted to belong to someone, to be told I was doing a good job; I wanted to be hurt and cleansed and freed from what I did last summer in Rome, and then held until this loneliness finally, finally went away—

But that was a child's wish, and I was no longer a child.

As St. Paul said, I had to set aside my childish ways.

Had I really thought I might have some kind of fairy tale with Mark Trevena? The man who owned a sex club fueled by blackmail and secrets? Who had done God only knew what for the United States government and had seemingly no remorse over it?

And what about me? Regular girls were allowed to fall in love, to hope for other people to love them back, but I was not a regular girl. I'd been promised to God too long ago, and my life had always been meant as a sacrifice.

That I'd hoped for more, hoped for affection and sex,

showed how frail and selfish I still was. How imperfect my offering to God remained. The books on saints weren't full of stories of people begrudgingly surrendering their lives to God or weeping over what they'd lost when they decided to follow him. They did it with glad hearts, and if they couldn't do it with a glad heart, then at least they did it with a quiet, noble one.

So Mark had lied last night, and weak, hopeless sinner that I was, I'd believed him.

But I couldn't find the most crucial thread of this—even after pushing aside the stinging humiliation, the hollow ache of rejection and loneliness, it eluded me.

"Why?" I asked. "I was the one who suggested we eliminate my hymen. I would have done it without—without all the things you said. Without you pretending."

Even now, all this time later, I still look back on how my voice trembled with unshed tears and I shake with shame. We are called to forgive, but how can you forgive someone for seeing one of the weakest versions of yourself? How can you ever forgive yourself for showing it to them?

It was only the city light from the window that revealed the way his hand flexed after I spoke. The tiniest shift of his fingers. But his face didn't change. And when he spoke, his voice was as cold as it had been the first day I'd heard it.

"I'm not willing to lose all that I could gain from this marriage to your father's whims, even if it means temporarily courting his paranoia. And all that I could gain will be severely compromised if you grow to hate me because you gave this up for as clinical a reason as assuring your father. If you had spread your legs with no motivation other than that —even if you'd gone back to your room and wedged your own fingers inside of yourself without me there—it would have forever been a mark in your ledger against this marriage. Against me. One more thing you thought you were stoically surrendering when you were actually only hiding from yourself how much it hurt to have taken away." He lifted a shoulder. "This way, you couldn't lie to yourself later and say your hand was forced. You wanted it as much as you've ever wanted anything physical. It was your choice."

"A choice informed by the lie you told me," I said. I hated that I was naked right now, that my voice was still quavering, but I wouldn't reach for the sheet or clear my throat. He wouldn't get my shame from me as well as my weakness—at the very least, I'd keep that one thing for myself. "How do you know that I won't hate you for making me believe that you wanted me? Making me believe you wanted me to belong to you?"

"A calculated gamble," replied Mark calmly. "But one I felt confident in taking, because I know you, Isolde Laurence. You'll always hate yourself first. When you look back on this, it will be yourself you want to burn alive; it will be your own choices you want to scourge yourself for. You might tell yourself that it's because you're so deeply sensible and logical that you know you could never control me or my actions, that it's only worth agonizing over your own behavior. And you'd be partly right. But there's a lot more to you than sense and logic, isn't there? You were born guilty; you were born feeling stained and ready to suffer for it. God found you before anyone else could, and so now you'll lay yourself on any altar you can find to atone for the sin of being alive when your mother is dead, for the sin of being mortal and therefore imperfect. For the sins you intentionally commit now in God's holy name."

My lips were open, my ribs were seizing, but the air wouldn't come. I couldn't seem to drag it back into my lungs, back into my blood.

"You can't—" I finally managed a short, sucking breath. "You can't know that."

He stepped close enough to touch me, turning so that the light from the window caught more of his face. There was pity in it when he said, "Of course I know it, Isolde. Just as I know you think to play the game with me, capturing my pieces on the board, just as I hope to move your father's. But I have played this game a lot longer than you and with people far more dangerous than you, and I will win every match, little wife, every bout, and I won't even need to try when I do it. I know everything about you and you know nothing about me. I am willing to do whatever it takes to get what I want, and you will always be shackled to what your God asks of you."

He reached out with the hand that wasn't in his pocket, his fingers lifting my chin. I stared at him stonily, willing him not to see the tears pricking at my eyes, the fast swallow of my throat.

"You are terrified that your soul will be damned to hell. And I no longer have one left at all."

I blinked at him, this cruel man I'd made an idol of, and he lowered his face, his mouth hovering just above mine.

"So you see? I am going to win. I will always win, not in the least because I know the game we are playing, and I know all the players, and I know the stakes. I will win because I've won before. I will win because I'll die before I lose."

His nose brushed mine, and then his lips ghosted over my own. My traitorous body responded instantly, craving more of him, his tongue and lips and everything.

"Decide what game you want to play, my honeysuckle queen," he murmured into my mouth. "And then play it like you mean it. Even if you know you'll lose anyway."

And with that, he dragged his mouth to my temple and buried his nose in my hair, inhaling me. I meant to step back, to twist away, but by the time I could convince my body to pull away from his, he was already moving out the door, in long, predatory strides that reminded me of every time I'd lost or surrendered to him. In the karate school, on the stage at Lyonesse. Tonight in the library.

Once I heard the elevator chime and its doors close, I sucked in a long, quivering breath and let out a shattered sob. The tears came hot and fast and awful, and I bent over, unable to stop the noises that came out of me, unable to stop the pain.

It hurt, it hurt, it hurt, a thousand times worse than his flogger, than his fingers inside me for the first time. It was bad enough that I'd been forced into this marriage, but to have fallen in love with him too? To have been played, tricked, and now abandoned?

It was just salt in the wound.

And for my naiveté, my unconscious arrogance—my making a false idol out of Mark Trevena—I deserved it. Wound, salt, and all.

THE DAYLIGHT WAS MAKING MY ROOM BRIGHT AND HORRIBLE by the time the tears stopped. I had ended up on the floor somehow, curled on my side, and I was dizzy when I stood. Dizzy and yet clear, so keenly, sharply clear.

Like the entire world was made of knives and for the first time I could tell the spines from the edges. The live blades from the dull ones.

Mark thought I would hate myself before I hated him? He thought I would lose any game I played against him? He might be older, stronger, the devil sent to scourge other devils, but I was Isolde Laurence, and I had been forged for years into a weapon to be wielded against devils exactly like him.

Maybe he had no soul left, but I would lock mine away, where no one could touch it ever again, and when we met again for our wedding, we'd meet as equals. I would get what I needed from him and Lyonesse's archives; he would get nothing that mattered from me. And one day, if God granted my prayers, he would feel the same crushing humiliation and heartbreak that I felt right now, naked and sore in my bedroom on a cold winter day.

I turned to leave for a shower, pausing as the thing Mark had been flipping between his fingers and then had dropped on my desk caught my eye. It was a holy card that my Uncle Mortimer had sent me after I'd come home from Rome. St. Julian the Hospitaller.

It read in swooping cursive underneath the prayer: *Tu me superbus.*

You make me proud.

And I would, I vowed. I would make everyone proud, no matter the cost to myself, no matter the pain.

My sins to save God's kingdom, after all.

fifteen

PRESENT DAY

"Are you ready?" my uncle asks.

I turn away from the window to see him standing behind me in his black simar and scarlet skullcap, his hands laced behind his back. He's framed by the grand dining room of Cashel House, the country manor just outside Wexford that's been handed down through the Cashels for generations. My mother is dead and my uncle can't own property as a cardinal priest, and so as the last Cashel standing, the manor is mine.

I've visited several times over the last two years, mainly under the pretense of overseeing an extensive renovation, but this time I came because I needed a few weeks on my own after my graduation from Columbia.

A few weeks before Mark came to collect his bride at long last.

Mortimer flew in from Rome two days ago to join me. For moral support, he said, although the last two days have been more about strategy than support. Mark and I have barely seen each other since that night in my penthouse—just the once for a fake collaring ceremony where he barely touched me and Dinah shuffled me into a car right after—and my uncle is eager for information at long last. Gossip, observations. Eventually, whatever treasures are inside Lyonesse's electronic archives, the payments rendered for joining Mark's depraved kingdom.

"Of course," I say evenly. "It's what we've been waiting for."

My uncle steps forward to join me at the window, and I turn to follow his gaze. Cashel House looks out over a cliff-hedged cove, the shallow waters a gorgeous turquoise against the darker, deeper blue. There is a summer storm scudding overhead, forbidding and restless.

"You have made me proud beyond measure these last few years," Mortimer says. His lilting voice is both serious and fond. "You've become everything I've hoped for and more. No matter what happens in your marriage with Mark, you've already brought God's kingdom such strength and cunning that your treasures in heaven will be countless."

I keep my eyes on the water. "Thank you." Years ago, it was all I wanted to hear, but now my heart's locked away, and my need for comfort along with it. A blade only needs sharpening, not encouragement. I don't need his reassurances in order to keep slicing.

"You will make me proud in your new role, I know. And now that you are officially employed by your firm, you will be able to travel all the more easily for your other tasks."

I nod. After my graduation, I formally accepted a role as an appraiser of religious art and artifacts for a firm owned by a friend of my uncle. And in order to properly appraise such things as they come on the market, I will of course need to travel. A very convenient job to have in my situation.

The window also looks out onto the drive, a narrow

stretch of fresh, white gravel between Cashel House and the sea. The road that will bring Mark to me any moment now.

I look back to my suitcases, packed and waiting by the door. I draw in a breath, then another, feeling my core muscles expand and contract. My breath and blood and bone, entirely under my control. It took every minute of the last two and a half years, but the Isolde who believed Mark Trevena when he said he wanted her is gone.

Play it like you mean it, he said to me before he left that morning.

Well, I'm here now. More than two years of barely sleeping, of running and lifting and training and sweating. More than two years of perfecting languages, of making contacts through my father and uncle's worlds, of getting flawless grades. Two years of answering my uncle's summons and making sure the wicked knew that God was watching.

Mark once talked about passing through doorways that couldn't be walked back through. I'd stepped over so many of those thresholds now that it was hard to remember who I was before. Not that it matters. That girl wouldn't have survived what's coming next.

"Why the yacht?" Mortimer muses as I angle myself to peer down the drive. Mark is close to being late. "Why not fly you home to Manhattan? What's his design here?"

I've asked myself the same question every day since Mark emailed me and announced he'd like to pick me up himself from Cashel House and sail me home on his yacht.

So we can spend some time together before the ceremony, the email blandly said, but it makes no sense. Mark doesn't respect me or desire me. I am a tool to him, a means to a shadowy end involving Laurence Bank. I don't believe he is interested in seducing me, and I don't think he would hurt or kill me. Not this early in the game.

So what then? Does he want to talk? Make sure our

stories are straight before we're plunged into the social churn of Manhattan and DC? Begin exchanging pieces of information like hostages?

"I don't know," I finally admit. I dislike not knowing. Not knowing is a way to end up dead. Or worse—defeated.

"Be careful," Mortimer murmurs just as a black car emerges at the end of the drive. My heart—horrible, stupid, horrible heart—gives an abrupt thud against my ribs before I manage to get control of it. I will cut it out before I allow it to want Mark Trevena again. "You know who he is."

"I will and I do."

Even Mortimer doesn't know everything Mark did in his previous life, largely because most of what Mark did in the CIA was never written down. Even so, the whispers and rumors I've heard about him in the last two and a half years are terrifying. He captured when he was working for the government; he maimed.

He killed.

One story claimed that he slid a knife between a harpist's ribs while they played at a symphony concert in Vienna. Another that he cut off someone's ears so they wouldn't hear their own screams.

I have no reason to doubt any of the stories, but I'm ready for the game. Mentally, physically. It doesn't matter how handsome he is, how rough his voice or possessive his touch. It doesn't matter that when he tied me up, when he touched me, I felt like my soul was newly washed and floating to the stars.

I'm ready this time.

Except when the car pulls up to the house and someone steps out of the driver's side door, it's not someone with dark blond hair and a cold, indifferent expression. It's someone I've never seen before.

My uncle and I both go to the front door, opening it just as the stranger is lifting his hand to grab the knocker.

"Hello," the stranger says, dropping his hand. "Mr. Trevena sends his regrets that he can't travel with Isolde himself to Manhattan. He's asked me to escort her instead."

He's as tall as Mark, layered with muscles under his plain but well-tailored black suit, with fair skin that's been lightly suntanned, dark, dark hair, and sage green eyes. He has a doll's long lashes, a straight nose, and a full mouth that is shaped in a subtle pout, giving him a look of perpetual melancholy.

His jaw, cheekbones, and forehead are flawless, without the ruggedness of Mark's features and all the beauty of a Victorian painting.

I have never seen him before in my life, and yet the moment his green eyes meet mine, it feels as if I'm coming home. My heart lifts, my pulse speeds. Something twists inside me like the honeysuckle pattern twists around my favorite knife.

"I'm sorry, I don't believe we've met," I say. Outwardly, I am composed and cool. Inwardly, it feels like a tide is coming in around my feet. One I can't stop.

Why are his eyes such a haunting shade of green? Like a garden that's been forgotten and then rediscovered in the fog?

"My apologies, Ms. Laurence; I should have introduced myself right away." He speaks with a polite but direct voice that's nonetheless musical for how controlled and American it is. He holds out his hand and I take it, something hot and sweet racing up my nerve endings as our palms touch, and then our fingers. His grip is warm and strong.

The tide is rising around my knees.

"I'm Mark's nephew-in-law and bodyguard," the stranger says. "Tristan Thomas, at your service."

To be continued in *Salt Kiss*...

the kiss is coming...

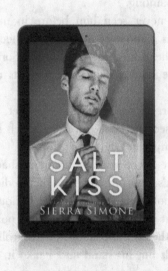

✓ Kinky MMF retelling of the Tristan and Isolde story
✓ Sexy bodyguard
✓ Morally gray hero
✓ Quietly lethal heroine
✓ Arranged marriage
✓ Wax play
✓ Horny pining!!!!

Tristan Thomas is lost.

After leaving the Army, the young former soldier is in limbo. Until, that is, he's hired by Mark Trevena, the owner of Lyonesse—DC's ultra-secret club—to be Mark's new body-guard. He's drawn into Mark's dark, seductive world of power and desire, and slowly drawn to Mark himself, even though Mark is everything Tristan knows he shouldn't want: cruel and wicked and shamelessly amoral.

But protecting Mark isn't Tristan's only duty: soon, Mark asks him to guard his soon-to-be bride as she travels home from Ireland on Mark's yacht. Tristan is jealous—and hurt to learn that the object of his obsession is engaged—but the soldier in him is made to obey orders, and he goes to fetch Mark's bride for him.

Isolde Laurence is nothing like Tristan expected, however. Young, quiet, and sharp, she's being pushed into this marriage by her family, and as the two travel back to America, Tristan finds himself fascinated with Isolde and the glimpses he gets of the lonely but determined woman behind her reserve.

And the fascination is mutual: one night, while sailing under the cold stars, they share a searing kiss.

From there, it's a fast fall into the forbidden.

But in Mark Trevena's world, the fall is only the beginning...

The Lyonesse trilogy is a queer, kinky contemporary retelling of the legend of Tristan and Isolde, set in the same world as the New Camelot series.

Readers will not have to read New Camelot to enjoy Lyonesse, although readers who enjoyed New Camelot will find all the things they loved about the trilogy here: MMF ménage, plenty of the angsty forbidden, and a sweeping retelling of a familiar story.

Salt Kiss will be available everywhere September 12th!

Salt Kiss will release LIVE on Amazon, but you can preorder from Apple Books, Google Play, Kobo, or Nook!

You can also preorder *Salt Kiss* in print wherever books are sold!

And the audiobook preorder is coming soon!

Stay up to date on all *Salt Kiss* news by subscribing to my newsletter via
www.subscribepage.com/saltkiss

Harvest of Sighs

Door of Bruises

Misadventures:

Misadventures with a Professor

Misadventures of a Curvy Girl

Misadventures in Blue

The New Camelot Trilogy:

American Queen

American Prince

American King

The Moon (Merlin's Novella)

American Squire (A Thornchapel and New Camelot Crossover)

High Spice Historicals:

The Markham Hall Series

The Awakening of Ivy Leavold

The Education of Ivy Leavold

The Punishment of Ivy Leavold

The London Lovers:

The Seduction of Molly O'Flaherty

The Wedding of Molly O'Flaherty

Far Hope Stories:

The Chasing of Eleanor Vane

The Last Crimes of Peregrine Hind

Co-Written with Laurelin Paige

Porn Star

Hot Cop

about the author

Sierra Simone is a USA Today bestselling former librarian who spent too much time reading romance novels at the information desk. She lives with her husband and family in Kansas City.

Sign up for her newsletter to be notified of releases, books going on sale, events, and other news at www.subscribepage.com/sierrasimone!

www.thesierrasimone.com
thesierrasimone@gmail.com